BURIAL GROUND

By the same author

**West of the Pecos
The Gold Hunters
The Gates of Hell
The Secret of Squaw Mountain**

BURIAL GROUND

ALAN C. PORTER

A Black Horse Western

ROBERT HALE · LONDON

© Alan C. Porter 1993
First published in Great Britain 1993

ISBN 0 7090 5154 9

Robert Hale Limited
Clerkenwell House
Clerkenwell Green
London EC1R 0HT

The right of Alan C. Porter to be identified as
author of this work has been asserted by him
in accordance with the Copyright, Designs and
Patents Act 1988.

Photoset in North Wales by
Derek Doyle & Associates, Mold, Clwyd.
Printed and bound in Great Britain by
WBC Ltd, Bridgend, Mid-Glamorgan.

To Mike and Lyn Wood:
long suffering in-laws.

ONE

The stage from Carson City to Redrock still had thirty miles to go when the Indians hit. They came yelling and screaming from the rocks, moccasined heels kicking into their horses flanks, rifles blazing. Deke Forest took one startled look over his shoulder and urged the team of six into a thundering gallop. Billy Jones having his first taste of riding shotgun for the Carson City Stage Line, turned on his seat and returned their fire. The swaying of the stage did little to help accuracy. By the same token the Indians shooting from the backs of galloping horses stood little chance of hitting the driver and his shotgun, but in this instance the Indians had applied stategy.

Up ahead where the high rocks crowded the trail on either side, Wolf and Coyote waited. As the stage came into view the pair took a bead on the driver and shotgun.

The bullet from Wolf's Henry smashed into Deke's chest, lifting him up and throwing him down on the stage roof. It took Coyote two shots from a Winchester he had taken from a dead prospector a week since to hit Billy, making the man's first trip his last.

Billy had squirmed into a kneeling position on the seat, back to the horses, when Deke's lifeless body, gouting spurts of blood, slammed down on to the roof of the stage. Billy had little time to contemplate the dead driver. He heard a bullet zing past his left ear. He didn't hear the one that snapped his spine and blew bloody gobbets of grey lung from his chest as it exited through a fist-sized hole. Billy was thrown forward, bounced back and fell between the stage and the galloping team. For the terrified passengers in the lurching, swaying stage, it was doubtful if they felt the extra bump or two as the iron-shod wheels pulped Billy's head into the dusty trail.

With no hand to guide them the team of six stretched their necks in a runaway gallop. On either side of the trail the rocks gave way to open range and a vast plain of yellow-flowered sagebrush, all horizons showing purple ridges of distant mountains. The Indians, dark hair flying, yelling and whooping in victory, slowly overhauled the stage. Two riders reached the lead horses and brought the team to a sweating, snorting, eye-rolling halt. Before the stage came to a stop wrapped in a cloud of dust, Running Dog had leapt on to its roof and with legs braced had stood triumphantly aloft, arms raised, rifle held high in victory. It was a short-lived victory for him. As the stage came to a shuddering halt a bullet gouged into his left eye and took away part of his skull in a gory explosion of blood, bone and brain.

He disappeared over the far side of the stage in a jerky tangle of arms and legs. Three more of the Indians went writhing and kicking into the dust before the remaining six, unable to see the hidden marksman, took to their mounts and galloped off.

Ashe watched from behind a rock pile as the Indians rode away from their abortive attack, a Winchester held in his hands. Minutes later, astride a big, black Morgan stallion, he headed towards the stage as the dazed, frightened passengers descended. One was a fat, white-suited drummer with a complexion to match his grubby suit. The other two were not so easy to classify.

A man and a woman. The man was garbed in a city-style suit, more befitting the streets of New York than the wilds of Nevada. He was short and plump and in his fifties. He observed Ashe's approach nervously from behind dark-rimmed spectacles, clutching a brown derby to his chest with thick, stumpy fingers. Thinning white hair lay wispily about his balding pate, but it was the woman who caught Ashe's eye.

Clad in a grey, ankle-length skirt with a matching top over a dark green blouse, her rich, chestnut hair had been swept back in a bun and hidden beneath a tiny, round, black hat. The slim face beneath the hat showed high cheekbones, large blue eyes and a wide, sensuous mouth. The beauty of the face that had seen no more than eighteen or nineteen summers momentarily took his breath away. He had grown so used to the coarse, painted faces of the saloon whores that he had forgotten other women existed. As he swung down from his horse, the rifle still clutched in one hand, the man stepped forward, a tense smile forming on his round face.

'We are indebted to you, sir. Lord knows what those heathen rogues had in store for us?' He glanced about fearfully. The man's accent was strange.

'Well it sure wasn't no invite to a Sunday school picnic,' Ashe replied drily.

'Such a wild country,' the man said. 'I am Professor George Little.' He marshalled his thoughts. 'And this is my daughter Constance.'

'It was a good thing for us you were in the vicinity, sir,' Constance spoke, her eyes appraising Ashe, offering a small hand that became lost in his great, rough paw. She felt a thrill flutter through her as she looked up into his tanned, stubble-chinned face with its tawny eyes and ringlets of dark hair tumbling about his ears from beneath a low crowned, black stetson.

Ashe was the kind of person people looked at twice and made sure they didn't upset him. Standing at seventy-six inches, shoulders broad beneath a red shirt overlaid by a tan, buckskin jacket, he wore a double-action Colt Lightning strapped low on his right hip. The leather of the holster was oiled and polished and cutaway for a smooth, fast draw. Just now his dark pants and boots were coated with dust.

'My pleasure ma'am,' Ashe replied touching his

hat brim. 'They call me, Ashe. Where you folks from?'

'England, Mr Ashe,' the man supplied.

'Just Ashe,' Ashe corrected with a faint smile. 'If'n I had a first name I reckon I've forgotten it by now.' So they were English. He remembered a man he had met in Denver one time. He had been English and spoke with the same clipped, precise tone.

'Well excuse a body for butting in, but shouldn't we be hightailing it outa here?' The fat drummer made his presence known. 'Seems t'me them Injuns could be back and Horace Jenks, that's me, would surely like to keep his hair on his head.'

Ashe regarded him coolly and Horace suddenly wished he had kept his mouth shut. He swallowed and licked his lips nervously.

'Man's got a point, folks. It's still a-ways to Redrock.'

Horace grinned with relief.

'That's the kinda talk I like to hear.' He pushed forward to climb aboard the stage.

'Not you, Horace.' Ashe's voice stopped him. The drummer's head snapped around and Ashe indicated upwards with his eyes. 'You ride shotgun with me.'

Horace's face paled a second time.

'I ain't no shotgun,' he wailed.

'You are this trip. You strike me as a fella who looks out for himself and that's just the right attitude for a shotgun. Climb aboard, folks.'

As the stage pulled out with Ashe in the driving

seat and his Morgan hitched behind, a pair of hate-filled eyes in a nut-brown face watched from the high rocks a mile to the west. Etched against the blue sky, Scar, the Shoshoni war leader, stood sentinel still. A warm wind blew across the desert stirring black hair that hung to his shoulders, a coloured headband keeping it from his eyes. When viewed from the right, Scar displayed a cruel yet handsome profile that matched the rugged, muscular proportions of his body. From the left his face was a mutilated ruin. Parallel scars ran in puckered welts from his ear, part of which was missing, and down across his cheek, the legacy of an encounter with a puma in his childhood. His own people had mockingly nicknamed him Scar and he had grown to manhood hating the name, hating the face that maidens shied from.

Gradually over the years, Scar became a name to be feared instead of the butt of a cruel mockery. In battle he proved himself a warrior and in challenging the best in his own tribe and beating them, their respect grew. Now he no longer hated the name Scar. It had become a symbol of his own strength and determination.

He had watched his young bucks shot down and those who remained flee like yellow dogs. He felt shame at their ignoble defeat, even more so when a single man emerged. Though distance hid the man's face, Scar recognized the build and buckskin jacket.

'Ashe!' The single name slid from his lips. He had encountered the big white man on more than one occasion and each time Ashe had come out the victor. The memory sent a bitter expression chasing across Scar's ravaged features. He raised a clenched fist as the stage pulled away. 'Ashe! You will die next!' he shouted hoarsely.

Oblivious to Scar's threat Ashe whipped the horses into a gallop and with an unhappy Horace Jenks at his side, headed towards Redrock. The remainder of the journey passed without incident and it was mid-afternoon that Ashe brought the stage into Redrock, trailing a wake of red dust against the distant ridge of the Sierra Nevadas. People gathered excitedly as Ashe brought the stage to a creaking halt outside the stage office.

Sheriff Clem Peters pushed his way through the crowd.

'Didn't know you drove for the stage line, Ashe,' he called up.

'Neither did I, Clem,' Ashe returned as he climbed down. 'There's a dead man on the roof. Indians.'

'The hell you say. Baldy, Willis, get that body over to the undertaker's.' He called two men from the crowd as Ashe joined him on the ground. Serious eyes in a moustachioed face studied Ashe. 'Scar?'

'They were Shoshonis right enough, but Scar wasn't with 'em. Figure he left it to the young bucks to see how they made out.'

'Damn that Indian. He's got the whole territory

stirred up,' Clem said with passion as he watched the passengers alight. 'Army sits on its blue ass and does noth ...' His eyes popped and words faded. 'What the hell have you got there, Ashe?'

A smile twitched Ashe's lips as the pair, the small professor in the lead, came towards them.

'Visitors from England,' Ashe replied and introduced them to the sheriff.

'I would like to say, Sheriff, that had it not been for Ashe's timely arrival, those savages would have butchered us by now,' the professor spoke up. 'I shall recommend his bravery to the stage line.'

'We sure wupped them redskins.' Horace, now on firm ground, fully recovered from the shock and with the protection of the town about him, bragged loudly and beamed at the crowd. These were potential customers, hot for news and to Horace that meant greater sales of "Doctor Morton's Liver Tonic" and more money in his pocket. 'Yes sir, I rode shotgun with Ashe an' I kin tell you folks ...' Horace pushed towards the crowd followed by an amused look from Ashe.

'Now, Sheriff, perhaps you would be kind enough to direct us to a reputable hotel,' the professor asked.

'Surely, Professor, ain't but the one in town anyway. Hey Otis, take these folks across to the hotel.' Clem called a thin, sallow-faced man from the crowd that was now breaking up as Horace went into his pitch.

'And if you would be kind enough to have our luggage sent over.'

'Luggage?' Clem tipped his hat back.

'Bags,' Ashe whispered.

'You heard the man, Otis, that's bags,' Clem delegated.

'Perhaps Ashe would like to join us for dinner, Father,' Constance suggested, smiling up at Ashe.

'Yes of course. We'd be delighted if you would join us, Ashe.' The professor beamed from behind his spectacles. 'Seven o'clock at the hotel. Come, Constance.' With that the professor moved off with Otis in the lead. Constance followed after a lingering look at Ashe.

'Delighted. Dinner.' Clem scowled suspiciously at Ashe. 'Is this some sorta wind up, Ashe? You got these folks to play a game?'

'No game, Clem. They're genuine,' Ashe laughed.

'The hell you say.' Clem massaged his chin. 'What the hell's a professor do an' how does he do it in Redrock?'

Ashe shrugged. 'If'n I find out I'll let you know.' With that Ashe moved to the rear of the stage, unhitched his horse and led it towards the livery.

I'm an archaelogist, Ashe,' the professor said expansively as the dinner plates were cleared and they waited for coffee.

In the hotel dining-room that also served as a restaurant to the town, the meal had been a pleasant, informal affair. Most of the talk had come from the professor asking questions about Ashe and the territory around them. It was only now that the man began to open up about himself.

'Sure is a mouthful o' a word, Professor,' Ashe said, none the wiser.

'What Daddy means,' Constance broke in with a laugh. 'He studies the past through remains left by our ancestors. Pottery, weapons, old ruins that have been deserted for hundreds of years.'

Ashe eyed her doubtfully.

'And a man gets paid for that?'

'Not on a commercial basis, Ashe, purely scientific,' the professor chuckled. 'To further the knowledge of man's progress through the ages before even the white man set foot on this great continent.' The professor nodded; Ashe was impressed. It was now a different Ashe to earlier. Bathed, shaved and in fresh, clean clothes, he felt more in keeping with polite society. Constance had changed into a long, blue dress and released her hair so it now flowed like burnished copper to her slim, pale shoulders. Ashe sat facing Constance with the professor to his left. The restaurant was half full. Behind the professor a big, half-curtained window looked out on to the night-shrouded street.

'Sounds real fine, Professor,' Ashe said. 'What are you hoping to find around Redrock?'

'Not Redrock; our destination is some distance to the north. A site called Spirit Canyon to be precise.'

Ashe stiffened.

'Hold on there, Professor, that's sacred ground to the Indians. It's the old Shoshoni burial ground an' they don't take kindly to folks, white or red, going there an' disturbing the spirits.'

'Come, Ashe; disturbing the spirits? Don't tell me you believe in ghosts and demons?' There was gentle mockery in the professor's voice.

'It's not me you gotta worry about. The Indians believe, an' that's what matters,' Ashe replied grimly.

'No need to worry, old boy,' the professor said confidently. 'I have official approval from your State Department to investigate the site. We came from England at the invitation of Boston University to study this site. Tomorrow we travel to Fort Davis where we will join up with Professor Boyde and his team from the university. I understand that a troop of cavalry and a guide have been placed at our disposal to get us safely to the location.'

'I just hope someone's told the Indians,' Ashe said stiffly.

'Are the Indians dangerous, Ashe?' Constance asked.

'You saw what they were like this morning, ma'am,' Ashe pointed out.

'A renegade group of trouble-makers, Ashe,' the professor scoffed. 'An unprotected stage with just civilians aboard. We will have an armed, military escort. I think we can forget about your Indians.' He smiled at Ashe.

'I wouldn't dream of telling you your business, Professor, but I reckon I know a mite more about Indians than you do. That ground's sacred to them. Army or not they ain't about to let you in there without a fight.'

'That we will have to find out,' the professor said firmly. 'The State Department have sanctioned this trip and the army have voiced no such qualms.' His tone softened. 'I appreciate your concern, Ashe, I'm sure it is well meant, but my mind is made up and I mean to go.'

'We mean to go, Father,' Constance pointed out mildly.

Ashe stared at her in horror, but made no comment until after the waitress had poured their coffee and moved away.

'You mean to say that you are going on this lunatic trip as well?'

'I didn't travel all this way to sit in some seedy hotel.' Her eyes flashed with annoyance at the thought. 'And I would hardly call it lunatic, Ashe,' she ended stiffly.

Ashe was about to reply. Instead he let his breath out in a sigh and relaxed. He could no more dictate their actions than they could his.

'Guess I spoke out of turn,' he apologized. 'Folks buy a man a meal then it ain't right he should be rude to them.'

The annoyance left her eyes and she laughed.

'I'm sorry too. I suppose it does look lunatic to others.'

'Constance,' the professor rebuked.

'Who's your guide?' Ashe asked between sips of coffee.

'Fellow by the name of Sampson,' the professor

said and Ashe nodded.

'Ezra Sampson. A good man.' At the same time Ashe wondered why Sampson was taking on such a suicidal job. The man was good enough to know that he would be walking into a death trap.

Conversation became more general, then before the group broke up, the professor asked, 'Perhaps you can help us, Ashe or recommend a reliable person to drive us out to Fort Davis tomorrow morning. Anyone who helps would be suitably recompensed for their time.'

'Don't need no recompensing, Professor. It's kinda on my way an' it'll be my pleasure to escort you and Miss Constance to the fort. I kin hire a rig from old Amos or would you prefer horseback?'

The professor grimaced at the thought.

'At my age I think a rig would be the thing,' the professor said and the group broke up laughing, but there was little to laugh about the following day when they arrived at Fort Davis, Constance driving the rig and Ashe riding alongside on his Morgan.

'We had a message from the Boyde party, they will be here tomorrow, but I'm afriad we have a problem,' Major Strong said as he met the group on arrival. 'Ezra Sampson, your guide, is dead. Got himself shot in a card game.'

'Oh dear, the poor man,' the professor said in dismay.

'And without a guide who knows the area I cannot let my men go with you. You do understand, sir?' the major hurried on.

'Is there no other guide available?'

The major's eyes drifted on to Ashe for a second, who was talking to a soldier.

'There is one man who probably knows the area better than Sampson ever did,' he said cautiously.

'Would he be willing to guide us?' the professor asked eagerly.

'That you will have to ask him yourself, sir.'

'How do I get in touch with him?'

'He brought you here, sir. It's Ashe.'

TWO

Within the wooden walls of Fort Davis, Ashe listened to the little professor, face giving nothing away.

'If you will undertake to be our guide, Ashe, I will offer the same deal as we made to Mr Sampson. One thousand dollars.'

Ashe's eyes flickered; now he knew why Sampson had agreed.

'Do yourself and your daughter a kindness, Professor, and go back to England. Forget Spirit Canyon,' Ashe said bluntly.

The professor's face became stubborn and his eyes flashed behind the glass circles of his spectacles.

'I take it, sir, that the offer does not appeal to you?' he said stiffly.

' 'Bout the size of it, Professor,' Ashe agreed, nodding.

'Then there is nothing more to be said. I thank you for your time and trouble, Ashe.'

Ashe looked at the stiff-backed major.

'Major, you know the country and the Indians.'

There was an appeal in Ashe's voice that was lost on the major.

'My hands are tied, Ashe.' He shrugged apologetically. 'The professor has all the required authorization needed.'

'Except from the Shoshonis.'

'A show of force will deter any ideas they might have about making trouble,' the major said with an indulgent smile at Ashe before turning to the professor. 'But the stipulation is that a suitable guide must accompany this proposed expedition. The area you intend to visit is largely unmapped. Without someone who has personal knowledge of the area, I cannot provide an escort.'

'This is outrageous,' the professor stormed. 'I have come thousands of miles to make a trip and I will not be thwarted.'

'I'm sorry, sir, but those are my orders. Now if you'll excuse me I have other work to attend to.' The major did not wait to be excused. With a curt nod he turned and strode away.

'Surely you can be persuaded, Ashe?' A note of desperation had entered the professor's voice. 'A further five hundred dollars. Fifteen hundred dollars to be our guide.'

'Save your breath an' your money, Professor.' Ashe was not tempted.

The professor scowled. He did not like to be beaten.

'As you wish, but I'll find somebody, of that you can be sure. Good day to you, sir.' The professor turned on his heel and marched away.

'You won't reconsider, Ashe?' Constance asked.

'Sorry, ma'am. It's a mighty tempting offer, but staying alive is more tempting.'

She gave him a last, lingering look, a sad half smile painting regret into her features, then turned and followed her father. A few moments later Ashe, astride his Morgan, rode out through the gates of the fort and headed west, back towards Redrock.

Within the warm shade offered by the overhang of the sutler's store, Lyle Skinner had watched and listened to the exchange of words between the small man and Ashe. His ears had pricked up at the mention of money. After watching the two break apart, Skinner went into the store, furious thoughts whirling through his head.

The smells within the warm interior as he passed the dry goods were a mixture of spices and tobacco. In different areas of the store certain smells dominated before they mingled and merged with others. Beyond the racks of calico and cotton dresses where racks of boots rose to the ceiling, the smell was predominantly leather. It became whiskey-flavoured smoke as the rear corner of the store opened into a small bar-room that had been built on to the rear of the store. But Lyle noticed none of these smells as he flopped down in a seat at a battered, round table. A small, dirty window above threw a dull light over the table and its other occupant.

Clay Skinner loked up as his twin brother, Lyle, sat down. Both men bore the same thin, stubble-lined features with lank, greasy hair spilling about their ears beneath high-crowned stetsons. Their range clothes were shabby and dirty, boots cracked and scuffed. Lean built, each was a mirror image of the other, even down to the dirt-grimed lines etched into the weathered skin of their faces. The only way to tell them apart was that Clay favoured gaudy, colourful shirts. He wore a candy-striped affair beneath a dark vest while Lyle preferred sombre single colours, brown or black.

Clay, arms folded and resting on the table top, lowered his gaze to an empty whiskey glass set before him.

'Shit, Lyle. I done spent my last dollar. What we gonna do fer money?' he whined miserably. The only prospect in view was what they always did at times like this; clean out the stables for a few lousy dollars. He hated stables and he hated stinking hoss-shit.

'Got me an idee,' Lyle replied softly, eyes flickering about. They were the only two in the bar.

'Well it'd better be more'n shovelling hoss-shit and piss,' Clay replied sourly.

'It's somethin' better, Brother,' Lyle replied. He leaned forward on folded arms until their faces almost met. 'How'd you feel 'bout ...?' He mentioned the sum of money he had heard offered by the small man to Ashe and Clay's eyes popped.

'Jesus, Lyle. We gotta kill someone?' he squeaked.

'Hush your mouth, stupid,' Lyle hissed angrily, staring around again. A bored barman had appeared and was mechanically polishing glasses with a grubby cloth. Speaking in low tones Lyle filled Clay in on what he had overheard and Clay's face dropped.

'You done flipped, Lyle? Hell, Spirit Canyon. That's a one-way ticket to a real hard death.'

'That's how I see it for a bunch o' greenhorns,' Lyle admitted casually, an evil grin stamping itself on his thin, mean face.

'An' anyone fool enough to be with 'em,' Clay growled.

'Mebbe, but I reckon mebbe not. Now listen up.' For the next few minutes Lyle whispered and Clay listened, his head nodding, face running a gamut of expressions.

'How we uns gonna do that with a bunch of soldier-boys tagging along?' he said finally.

'Got me another idee, Brother,' Lyle said smugly. 'Let's go a-visiting.'

Constance did not like the two men who now invaded the quarters the major had provided for herself and her father. The men were dirty and stank of sweat, body odours and whiskey.

'Like I wus saying, sir,' Lyle spoke in his most servile and ingratiating voice, hair clawing down over his forehead and into his eyes as he held his hat against his chest. 'I heard you wus looking for a guide to take you out to Spirit Canyon. Me an' my brother, Clay, we done know that area better'n most. Ain't that a fact, Clay?'

'The pure truth, Lyle,' Clay lied glibly and at the same time mentally undressed Constance with leering eyes.

'What credentials can you produce to verify what you say?' the professor asked pompously and both men eyed each other in puzzlement.

'What my father means is can you prove what you say?' Constance broke in.

Lyle scowled from one to the other.

'You calling we uns liars?' His eyebrows rose and knitted together.

'We are not calling anyone liars, Mr Skinner,' the professor placated hastily. 'Just asking for some reasonable verification that you will be able to guide us there and back in safety.'

'Wouldn't be offering if'n we couldn't,' Lyle replied sulkily.

'That's not enough,' Constance flashed back and in the background Clay smiled wolfishly. She sure was a sassy bitch. It'd be real pleasure going belly-to-belly with that one.

'They don' issue see-tifikates if'n that's what you mean,' Lyle growled angrily. His temper was on a short fuse and the girl's constant butting in had made him reach its limit. His thoughts towards Constance were not as carnal as Clay's, but just as basic. He'd like to put a bullet between her damned eyes.

'Constance, will you kindly keep out of this,' the professor barked and Constance, rebuffed, pouted and with a sniff left the room. The professor smiled nervously. 'She means well.'

'They allus do,' Lyle remarked darkly. 'But this is man's business an' women got no call to be poking their noses in it. Like I said, you wanna get to Spirit Canyon; we kin get you there. I allus say, two guides is better'n one.'

'How much do you charge for your services?'

'It's dangerous country out there that's fer sure. You offered old Ezra a thousand dollars. Reckon it'd be fair to add another five hundred to that for the two of us.' He made no mention of the same offer he'd overheard made to Ashe, so he knew the old man was willing to pay that.

The professor chewed his lip. He was on the horns of a dilemma, torn between a dislike of the two men and his desire to go to Spirit Canyon. Desire won.

'I'll speak to my partner when he arrives tomorrow. If he's in agreement then you are hired.'

'Fair enough,' Lyle agreed. He didn't like it really, but if he pushed too hard he might push himself out.

'One thing I ain't too sure 'bout an' that's having army along.' Lyle shook his head and looked at Clay.

'Could be real trouble,' Clay came in on cue.

'Why do you say that?' the professor asked.

Lyle pursed his lips and blew air.

'Fact is, might have to put up the price if'n they were to come along.' He nodded gravely.

'I don't understand?' The professor looked one to the other.

'Yuh gotta know Indians. Ain't that right, Clay?'

'That's the truth, Brother,' Clay agreed.

'You go on their land wi'a passel of soldier-boys an' they ain't gonna know if'n you mean peace or war. Stan's to reason they's gonna get a mite proddy. Now you go in alone, take a few trinkets to trade an' why,' Lyle smiled, 'them redskins'll be more'n happy to let you visit Spirit Canyon.' He held his breath and waited for the professor's reaction.

'Makes sense,' came the reply after the thoughtful silence. It made a lot of sense to him to go as a friend. The presence of an armed escort would only antagonize the Indians. 'What about this Scar chappie?'

'Red or white, there's always gonna be a bad'un stirring up trouble. Soldier-boys'll catch up with that no-good soon enough. Ain't no cause to worry 'bout that redskin.'

The professor nodded.

'Nothing's been settled on this yet, Skinner. I'll have to talk to Professor Boyde tomorrow and we'll make the decision between us.'

'Tha's right, you sleep on it,' Lyle agreed easily. 'we'll be here come sun up if'n you want us. Come on, Clay.' With no further pressing, Lyle bundled his brother from the room.

'Are we in or out?' Clay demanded as they walked across the compound.

'Depends on how bad that fella wants to git to

Spirit Canyon an' it sure seems a powerful want to me,' Lyle said. 'It's that damn girl o' his who might spike it for us. We'll find out tomorrow.' At that moment Constance's objection to the unsavoury brothers was falling on deaf ears.

'That they smell is hardly a criteria to refuse to employ them,' the professor said airily as he unbuttoned his waistcoat.

'I don't trust them, Father.'

'I don't intend to jeopardize our chances of reaching Spirit Canyon on your whims, Constance,' he flared. 'What I am willing to do is find out what the good major thinks of the two before I make my final decision. Now I consider the matter closed.'

'The Skinner boys. Just a couple of no-account drifters. Do a little work around the fort when they need money.' It was after a meal that the major had laid on for them that evening, that Constance broached the subject of the Skinners.

'But are they trustworthy?' Constance asked.

' 'Bout as trustworthy as a rattler that's been stepped on. Have they been bothering you, ma'am?'

'They have offered their services as guides,' the professor cut in and the major's eyebrows arched.

'That's a first. They generally shy away from work if'n they can.'

'But would you recommend them?' Constance persisted, earning a disapproving glare from her father.

'No ma'am. They're a lazy shiftless pair, need watching all the time.'

'Not the sort in whose hands you'd place your life?'

'That's a fact,' the major agreed and Constance threw her father a triumphant look. He would have to take notice of her now, but the triumph dissolved at her father's next words.

'Would they be able to get us to Spirit Canyon, Major?'

'Heard tell they know the area, but I wouldn't recommend them.'

The professor nodded.

'It has been suggested that a military presence would not be necessary and that is something I would agree with. Don't get me wrong, Major. I have nothing against you or your men, but a show of force could lead to hostility. If we show the Indians that we mean no harm then they are more likely to accept us.'

The major rubbed his chin and eyed the professor.

'Tha's one way to look at it, Professor,' he agreed guardedly. 'But not one I would endorse in these troubled times. You had a run in with them yourself that could have had a very different ending had not Ashe happened along. I reckon you'd be ill advised to go without a military escort, but I can't force one on you.'

'Your advice is noted, Major. I shall take it up with my colleague, Professor Boyde, when he arrives and together we will formulate an agreement of how best to tackle this expedition.'

Much later, after the two had returned to their quarters, Constance turned to her father.

'You've already made up your mind, haven't you?' she said reproachfully.

'About what, dear?' He smiled innocently.

'We don't have an escort when we leave here with those awful Skinners.'

'Force only begets force,' he said loftily. 'The Skinners may have a hygiene problem, but we are not hiring them for cleanliness.' He chuckled. 'One thing you would do well to remember, Constance: once we set out, water will become far too precious to waste on washing facilities and that means we shall probably end up as odorous as the Skinners. Now get to bed, child. Tomorrow is going to be a busy day.'

There were six of them, young Shoshoni bucks, faces daubed with paint, hair swept back and the anticipation of making a kill shining in their eyes. The six who had remained alive after the attack on the stage. They moved silently over the buff-coloured, sun-baked rocks, clutching hunting bows of seasoned juniper. Against their naked backs lay a quiver full of arrows while at their waists hung knife and tomahawk. These were the old weapons of death before the white man came with his gun. These were all the six were allowed. Scar insisted this at their public humiliation where they were denounced as cowards and squaws and driven from the tribe. Now they had to earn the right to be called men and allowed back into the tribe. They had to kill the one called Ashe who had brought this shame down on them. Bring back his head for all to see using only the weapons they now carried.

Wolf and Coyote led, their keen ears picking up the chuckle and gurgle of water dancing over a pebble bed and the hiss of falling water. They were close now. Wolf motioned all down and they squirmed, belly to the hot rocks the last few yards, until they could look down into a deep gully that cut through the low hill range, thirty miles south-east of Redrock.

Once a mighty torrent of water had rushed, roaring, foaming and seething through the hills, cutting this gully. Now the water was just a shallow trickle of flashing silver along the bottom: a fifty-foot stretch from where the stream emerged, head height, from the rocks to where it disappeared underground again.

The sides of the gully were clothed in a ragged shawl of brush and sage. A stand of cottonwood clustered at the end where the stream disappeared to continue its journey underground. A few scrub oak and pinon pine rubbed woody shoulders here and there along the stream edge. Close to where the water tumbled from the rocks a big, black Morgan stallion grazed contentedly on a patch of grass.

Ashe, shirt off, crouched at the water's edge midway between the waterfall and the cottonwoods with a miner's shallow gold-pan. It was here he panned enough gold to feed and clothe himself. It was not rich pickings. The back-aching work was long and tedious and the yield small, but it afforded him the freedom he desired: to be his own man and not a servant of others.

Sweat sheened Ashe's upper body and itched a tickling path down his spine. It was four days since he had left the fort and the Littles. He wondered idly if they were still there. The professor had struck him as a mule-stubborn cuss who would not give up without a fight. He just hoped the little Englishman would not throw caution to the wind and strike out for Spirit Canyon without a guide, but then he dismissed the idea. Without a guide it would be impossible to find and he doubted the man was that suicidal. He'd swing by the fort in a couple of days and find out.

Ashe was conscious of the bird song coming from the stand of cottonwoods. He was even more conscious of the heavy silence when it stopped suddenly.

THREE

Ashe gave no outward reaction that he had noticed anything different, but inwardly he was tense. He continued to pan, a tingle of anticipation invading his body.

A minute passed and then another. Slowly the bird song started up again. Something had spooked them. An animal or man up in the rocks, now lying doggo. Ashe guessed man or men and mighty patient men, Indians! The sweat that coated his brow had little to do with the heat. He was out in the open, the only cover lay some ten feet away to his right in the form of a twisted-armed scrub oak. His rifle was with his saddle that was perched on a boulder near to where the Morgan was grazing. His only weapons were his Colt Lightning on his right hip and a thick-bladed hunting knife on his left. He strained his ears above the natural sounds of the gully to pick up any telltale sounds of furtive movement, but he heard nothing. It had to be Indians: a white man would have given himself away by now.

He continued panning for a few seconds more

then rose on creaking knees, tipping the silt from the pan before tossing the vessel down. Arching his spine he dug his fingers into the aching muscles in the small of his back, acting like a man just easing the cricks of toil from his bones. Through slitted eyes he observed the far rim of the gully and saw the blurred image rise against the sky as Coyote, wanting to claim the honour of killing Ashe, came to his feet.

Arrow nocked, hawk-feather flight touching his bronze cheek, Coyote swung the strained bow on the figure below. He had but an inch or two left before releasing the arrow. Even with a gun ready a man would have difficulty beating the flying arrow. With it holstered a man would have no chance. This thought went through Coyote's mind as he released the arrow.

Ashe snapped his eyes open and the blurred image sprang into clarity. Ashe's reaction was fast and automatic. He drew and fired, diving to the right in what seemed a single action. The arrow from Coyote's bow hummed harmlessly above Ashe; the bullet from Ashe's Colt Lightning was less kind. It tore into Coyote's body just below the sternum and made a gory exit hole in his back that jetted blood and fragments of shattered vertebrae into the air. Coyote spun and went down screaming and writhing on the sun-heated rock. He squirmed in agony as the scream died to a harsh, bubbling gurgle and blood pumped from his open lips and pooled on the flat surface. He died a few seconds later.

Ashe hit the ground and did a forward roll, sharp fragments of rock digging painfully into his bare back. He came to his feet and impetus carried him forward, propelling him face down behind the stunted oak as an arrow thudded into its spindly, deformed trunk. Another passed above him and clattered against the rocks. Squirming into a kneeling position he pumped two quick shots at darting shapes on the gully rim, missing both times.

Stones and loose earth rattled from the gully wall behind and above him. He threw himself down on his back, an arrow burying itself in the ground scant inches from his ribs. Wolf had sent two men on a flanking movement to get around behind him before Coyote's death. The Colt Lightning bucked and roared in Ashe's hand. A figure looking down from above caught the bullet under the chin. Its exit opened the top of the man's head like a giant rose. The man vanished from sight.

Whooping and yelling Wolf led the two braves remaining with him over the rim of the gully, slithering in clouds of dust down the steep slope across the stream. Bows discarded, the three had filled their hands with knife and tomahawk and now charged towards Ashe. Wolf had counted the bullets fired and knew that only two remained in the gun. Counting the brave who still remained on the gully rim above Ashe, there were four Indians and with no time to reload, Ashe could only kill two more before the others were upon him.

A brave to Wolf's left cried out and clutched at a

flat stomach, blood pumping redly between his splayed fingers as he attempted to plug the hole that had appeared there. His legs collapsed beneath him and he splashed face down into the water and lay still. Weaving left and right, Wolf felt a sting of fiery pain as Ashe's last bullet cut a furrow across his right, upper arm. The smarting pain became overlaid with triumph as Wolf yelled in his own tongue, 'The white man's gun is empty!'

As the hammer clicked uselessly on an empty chamber, a cold wash of fear rolled over Ashe. He reholstered the empty gun and drew his knife. Above him Dancing Cloud, seeing the others close in on Ashe, tossed his bow aside and ran along the gully rim, that was almost sheer rock at this point, looking for a place to scramble down. By this time Wolf and Singing Bird were closing in on either side of Ashe. Ashe grabbed up a short length of dead branch to act as a second weapon as he backed to the gully wall. His eyes flickered from one to the other. Beyond Wolf's smiling face, Dancing Cloud had found a place to climb down and was now running to join his brothers.

'You die, white eyes. I, Wolf will cut your heart out and feed it to the crows,' Wolf gloated. He spoke mission-school English, drawing Ashe's attention. Singing Bird took his chance and threw himself forward, knife and tomahawk ready, yelling his blood-curdling cries. Ashe half turned to meet the challenge, blocking the descending tomahawk with the branch, knife blades locking together where blade and hilt met. Singing Bird fell silent as the two strained against each other in a trial of strength.

Given time it was a trial that Ashe would have won for he was a head taller and shoulder wider than his opponent, but time was something he did not have. From the corner of one eye he saw Wolf leap forward. tomahawk raised.

Ashe brought his right knee up hard between the Indian's legs. Singing Bird buckled forward, pain greying his face and filling his eyes. Ashe twisted the branch against the tomahawk and flipped it from the man's grasp. Aware of Wolf's closeness Ashe swung Singing Bird in his path, using the branch as a bar beneath his chin to force his head up. Wolf was already committed to the blow that should have cleaved Ashe's head in half, instead Singing Bird got in the way.

With a sharp crack of bone the blade of Wolf's tomahawk split open Singing Bird's skull and buried itself deep within his brain. Ashe shoved the twitching body against Wolf and grabbed up the fallen tomahawk, backing as Wolf parried the lifeless body aside.

'You'll have to do better'n that,' Ashe taunted Wolf as Dancing Cloud reached Wolf's side.

'You will not talk so bravely with your head on a pole,' Wolf snarled back.

'Happen it would be a mite difficult,' Ashe agreed.

Dancing Cloud dashed forward, the tomahawk flying from his hand, the metal head flashing in the sunlight. Ashe hurled himself backwards hitting a patch of soft sand with his shoulders. Dancing Cloud yipped and threw himself on to Ashe, but the smile of triumph became a mask of pain as he landed on Ashe's knife, his own impetus driving the blade to the hilt into his stomach. The Indian gave a keening cry and jerked himself up and fell sideways, dragging the knife from Ashe's hand. His legs kicked in death convulsions as blood pumped from his mouth.

Ashe scrambled to his feet, his chest splashed with droplets of scarlet; he still held the tomahawk.

'Jus' you an' me now, fella,' he grated from a dry throat.

Wolf stared hatefully at Ashe, tensed his body as though to spring, but the fight had gone out of him. Five braves lay dead and it should not have been so. He backed away as with a last convulsive kick Dancing Cloud lay still.

'It is not over yet, white man. We will meet again,' Wolf cried then turned and loped away.

Ashe watched him go before tossing the tomahawk aside and retrieving his knife from Dancing Cloud's body. Trembling, chest heaving, Ashe washed the knife and himself in the stream and returned to where the Morgan waited. Suddenly the solitary life had turned sour. He had the urge to surround himself with a saloon and make friends with a whiskey bottle, perhaps dally with a girl. He needed company.

The sun was setting over Redrock, painting the

collection of white, clapboard buildings red and filling the alleyways with purple shadow, as Ashe left his horse at the livery and headed for the saloon. Sheriff Clem Peters found Ashe, some time later, sitting in a corner seat with a half-full bottle of whiskey set before him on the table.

'Celebratin' or grievin'?' he asked with a smile as he hooked a chair clear of the table with his foot and sat down. Ashe sent the potman for a glass for Clem. The saloon was just over half full, the greatest crush of people bellied against the bar. Smoke wreathed the rafters in a grey haze and coiled lazily about the hanging oil lamps. A number of gaudily dressed women wandered from table to table while a piano player in a yellow vest thumped out a tune on a piano that badly needed tuning, the discordant notes demanding, but not getting any attention above the hubbub of voices.

'Had a run-in with some of Scar's boys today.'

'Then I guess it must be a celebration seein' as you're still here,' Clem replied lightly. 'What happened?'

The potman brought the glass as Ashe unfolded his tale.

'Figured they were the young bucks who attacked the stage. Guess I was seen and Scar sent them out to get me. Had they been old hands it would probably be me lyin' in the dirt now,' Ashe concluded darkly.

'It's 'bout time the army did somethin' 'bout that Injun,' Clem grumbled as he splashed a shot of whiskey into his glass. Ashe's reply was halted by the arrival of a woman in a red silk dress, the top cut so low that it didn't seem possible it could hold in her generous figure. With hands on hips she smiled down at Ashe, red-painted lips stretched wide, blue eyes dancing with merriment beneath corn-coloured hair that flowed silkily to her bare shoulders.

'Hey, Ashe, you lookin' for some company, female company?'

Ashe squinted up at her a smile tugging at his lips.

'Hell, Suzie, that might be an offer I can't refuse later on.'

'Well, don' you forget now. You an' me together sure do make sweet music.' Her eyes fell on Clem. 'How 'bout you, Sheriff?' she leaned forward allowing Clem an inviting view of deep cleavage. 'Young Ginny over there is hot to lay a real lawman.'

Dragging his gaze from her ample breasts, Clem looked solemnly into her eyes.

'Being a duly appointed peace officer, I wouldn't be able to uphold the law from a bed.'

Suzie smirked.

'You leave the upholding to Ginny, Sheriff. She's a real good hand at that.' Suzie threw back her head in a coarse, bleating laugh that had heads turning in their direction and to Ashe's amusement, Clem's face coloured. The sheriff was saved any further embarrassment by the arrival of Rusty. Age had removed every hair from his head, but nature had seen fit to bless the old prospector with a full, bushy ginger beard.

'Hey, Suzie, how 'bout going a round or two wi'

me? I might be old, but I ain't dead.' He gave a toothless smile.

'You would be after two rounds wi' me, old-timer,' Suzie roared for the benefit of the smiling onlookers. She looked wistfully at Ashe. 'See you later, mebbe?'

'Mebbe,' Ashe replied.

Her glance fell wickedly on Clem.

'Remember, Sheriff, a man upholding his own ain't having as much fun as he could have with a women helping him.' Laughing, Suzie turned to the ever hopeful Rusty and grabbed a handful of his beard. 'You damn old, billy goat. Happen you'll tickle a girl to death. I'll buy you a drink an' then you kin tell me where all your gold's at.' She led him away.

Clem took a deep swallow from his glass.

'Tha Suzie's getting a mite too sassy for her own good. One of these days she's gonna find herself in the pokey doing a twenty-four hour stretch for being a public nuisance. Why, you shoulda heard what she said to the banker an' he had his wife wi' him at the time.' He shook his head, but there was a smile on his face.

Ashe laughed, starting to relax.

'Shouldn't be too quick to slap her in jail, Clem. Jus' might happen that Ginny'll be along visiting.'

'Now don' you start, Ashe,' Clem warned, but was still smiling. 'Hey, almost forgot. That professor fella an' his daughter are gone.'

'Back to England?'

'Spirit Canyon. Coupla soldier-boys brought the

rig back a day or ago. Hear tell they picked up a coupla guides an' lit out.'

Ashe stiffened.

'Guides?' he barked, tawny eyes on Clem.

Clem squirmed a little in his seat.

'You ain't gonna like it much. The Skinner boys.'

'An' no one tried to stop 'em?'

'Seems that nothing stops that English fella once he's on the prod. 'Nother thing; they lit out without an escort.'

Disbelief filled Ashe's eyes. He banged a fist down hard on the table-top making bottles and glasses dance and drawing curious glances from the nearer patrons.

'Of all the stupid, mule-dumb things to do. What the hell was the major up to letting 'em go without an escort?'

'The professor reckoned that an army escort would only antagonize the Indians an' it was better to show a peaceful front.'

'The Skinners were happy to ride without an escort?'

'They suggested it, from what I hear.'

'Those boys are up to somethin',' Ashe said bleakly. 'They'd be the first to hide behind a blue uniform an' they sure as hell wouldn't ride all that way unprotected.' Ashe stared broodingly at the table top. 'Fact is they wouldn't ride all that way.' He came to his feet and Clem's eyes followed him.

'What are you saying, Ashe?'

'The professor was offering mighty tempting money. Figure the Skinners to take the money an'

Burial Ground

ride off, leaving them to the Indians.'

'Hell, Ashe, a man wouldn't do that.' Clem sounded horrified.

'The Skinners would,' Ashe said grimly. 'I'd better get out to the fort. Need to convince that blasted desk major to send a troop of men out after 'em.'

'Now hold on a spell. Major ain't gonna send men out in the middle of the night an' ain't gonna be too pleased to be got outa bed by you. Get some rest and leave at sun-up.'

In fact Ashe arrived at the fort as the first grey light of day was breaking to the east. The major wasn't best pleased to be faced by an irate Ashe before breakfast.

'I can't force people to accept an escort. My orders were to provide one if required,' the major said testily when he could get a word in. 'And to put your mind at rest, Lieutenant Rolf is patrolling with Company C in the Lone Butte area. It's on the wagon party's route. If they run into any trouble the lieutenant will bring them back safely. He's due in later today.'

Ashe fretted about the fort for the remainder of the day and it was not until late afternoon that the lieutenant and Company C returned. Tired and dishevelled, they were a battered looking troop the lieutenant led in. Three men were ominously draped over their saddles and a few more displayed bloodied bandages. As the doctor and his orderlies came running, Lieutenant Rolf slid wearily from his horse and drew himself to attention saluting the major.

'At ease, man. For God's sake what happened?'

'Scar and his men, sir. Hit us a mile south of Lone Butte early this morning. Three men dead and six injured.'

'Did you see anything of the wagon party that left here earlier in the week?' Ashe stepped forward.

'No. Saw sign that they'd passed that way, mebbe two days ago.'

'How many with Scar?' the major asked.

'Thirty, forty. All painted for war an' toting Winchesters; every last one of 'em.'

'What were they doing at Lone Butte?' the major asked.

'Only one thing they could be doing, sir, following the wagon party an' they ain't in no hurry. Got all the time in the world. One thing, sir, the Winchesters they carried were all box new. Somebody's supplying 'em.'

'Damn hell,' the major breathed.

'What about the wagon party, Major?' Ashe broke in impatiently.

'Dismissed, Lieutenant. Tend to your men and we'll talk later.' He turned to Ashe as Rolf turned away. 'There's very little I can do, Ashe. I don't have the men to chase Scar across the desert.'

'But you just can't leave 'em to be slaughtered,' Ashe objected strongly.

'They may be dead already,' the major said bluntly. 'It's too late for them. I'm sorry to sound callous, but my immediate concern is for the towns and ranches in this area. With Scar and his men supplied with Winchesters they could be getting ready for a big attack. I've got to be ready.'

Ashe stared hotly at the man then turned abruptly on his heel and strode quickly towards his horse.

Clem looked up startled as later, Ashe burst noisily into his office, face angry. In clipped, rapid words Ashe relayed what had transpired at the fort.

'I need to borrow your two Remingtons, Clem, an' another Winchester,' Ashe concluded, eyes drifting to the gun rack on the wall.

Clem's eyes widened.

'You ain't figuring on going out there, Ashe? The major's right, they could already be dead.'

'There's a whole heap o' difference between *could* an' *are*. Figure Scar'll bide his time. Play with 'em a little then kill 'em an' that might just give me the edge I need.'

Clem shook his head in wonderment.

'You're crazy, Ashe, you know that?'

'Who's arguing. Do I get the guns?'

'You know you do.'

'I'll be back for 'em, few more things I gotta get yet.' Ashe was about to turn away when Clem waved a telegraph slip in the air. 'Looks like you were right 'bout the Skinners. Had this message from the sheriff over in Beasely. Seems the Skinners are in town with plenty of money to spend. He knows them boys from old an' wired me to find out if there had been any robberies in Redrock lately.'

'What did you tell him?'

'Ain't sent the reply yet. Was on my way to do it when you arrived. I'll wire him to hold those boys 'til we find out what's going on.'

'Just tell him no.'

Clem's eyes narrowed.

'What are you up to, Ashe? I thought you wanted to speak to those boys.'

'I intend to,' he said darkly and disappeared out of the door.

FOUR

Clay Skinner pushed what dry twigs he could find into the ashes of the previous night's fire, fanning them, with his hat. As he hunkered there he had drawn a ragged blanket about his thin shoulders in an attempt to keep out the early morning chill.

'Damn son-of-a-bitch wood is damp,' he moaned to Lyle who still lay huddled in his bedroll. Around them a damp, morning mist flowed from the trees. 'Shoulda stayed in Beasely for the night,' he continued grumpily.

'Will yer quit bellyachin',' Lyle snapped from his bedroll, sitting up sleepily. 'I told' you. That there sheriff was looking at we uns pretty damn close. Figure it was best fer us to be on the move afore he started getting real nosey.' He dragged a two-thirds empty whiskey bottle from his bedroll, belching loudly as he pulled the cork, then jammed the neck of the bottle into his mouth.

'Hey, gimme some of that, Lyle.' Clay made a grab for the bottle, but Lyle jerked it from his mouth, dribbling whiskey down his stubble-blackened chin as he held the bottle out of Clay's reach.

'You git that damn fire going, boy.' Lyle sang out and took another pull on the bottle, then with a grin tossed the almost empty bottle to his scowling brother.

'Shit, Lyle you ain't left much,' Clay complained.

'If'n you don't want it then I'll have it back,' Lyle replied and Clay quickly drained the bottle and tossed it into the undergrowth. The twigs on the fire were beginning to crackle into life. Lyle climbed out of his blankets and relieved himself noisily against a nearby rock.

'How much money we got, Lyle?' Clay, hunkered by the fire again, asked as he set a blackened coffee pot in the flames. It was a question Clay had asked a dozen times. He knew the answer, but liked to hear it told him and Lyle played along with him.

'Close on three thousand dollars, boy.' Lyle returned to the fire and squatted down, hands stretched to the small flames. 'Easiest pickings we've ever had. Like takin' candy from a kid. That's why we gotta be real careful till we uns is away from here. Once we gets to New Mexico we'll have ourselves a real, good time. Best whiskey, best women.'

'Lordy, that's my idee of heaven,' Clay said dreamily. Just then there came a rustling from the undergrowth behind Clay. Clay snapped his head around while Lyle drew a Smith and Wesson.

'Some damn animal,' Lyle muttered throatily a minute or so later, reholstering the gun and settling down.

'Are you sure that wagon party ain't gonna make it, Lyle?' Clay sounded anxious and Lyle gave him a withering look.

'Men that know the area have died out there. Ain't no way them city dudes is gonna make it. We drove their mules off an' salted their water barrels. They's as good as dead.'

'Shoulda kilt 'em,' Clay said.

'No need. Injuns was watching us, seen 'em a coupla times. 'Sides it wouldn't do for an army patrol to find 'em full o' .45s. Injuns'ud make a better job o' it.'

Clay gave a giggle.

'Sure woulda liked to have given that sassy Constance a good time. Damn bitch coulda done wi' a real man up her skirts.'

'Ain't likely to get that from you pair of scum.'

The sudden voice coming from the mist startled both men. In trying to turn from a crouching position, Clay ended up sitting in the dirt. Lyle came to his feet, hand hovering close to his Smith and Wesson, but he did not draw it. His eyes popped as he saw the owner of the voice.

'Ashe!' The name burst thickly from his lips.

Ashe stood on the edge of the trees where only moments earlier the two men had heard sounds that they had attributed to some animal. A brown poncho draped Ashe's upper body. He held a shotgun casually in his left hand, butt resting against his hip. The poncho was hitched up on his right hip to reveal the Colt Lightning ready to use.

'So you left 'em to die? Left 'em for the Indians

to butcher?' Ashe's voice rang out coldly. 'Ain't a thing a man'd do, but then you Skinners ain't men.' His tawny eyes flashed in the shadow cast by the brim of his hat.

'No need to mean-mouth us, Ashe,' Lyle said sullenly.

'Took their money, salted their drinking water an' ran their mules off,' Ashe repeated what he had overheard, suppressed fury clipping his words.

Lyle licked his lips. heart thumping wildly in his chest, hand hovering nervously above the butt of his gun. He forced a smile.

'Ain' no need to get riled, Ashe. We'll cut you in for a third. Thousand dollars. How does that sound?'

'Like you've just dug your own grave,' came the bleak reply.

Lyle went for his gun. Ashe let the shotgun drop forward, firing as Lyle's gun cleared leather. The boom of both barrels erupting at once deafened Clay, causing him to cover both ears with his hands. The butt of the shotgun kicked back into Ashe's hip, but he was braced for it. Lyle was lifted off his feet and thrown back, clothing and flesh stripped from his chest in a scarlet cloud. For an instant his ribs showed whitely, then they shattered as the heavy twelve gauge punched a large hole and exploded heart and lungs into a red, pulpy mess.

Clay, white faced, leapt wildly to his feet, jabbing his hands at the mist hidden sky.

'Jesus, Ashe, why'd you do that?' His voice was shrill and uneven.

'Where'd you leave the wagon party to die, ass-hole?' Ashe's eyes settled on the man.

'Maze Canyon. It was Lyle's idea,' Clay wailed. 'I ain't pulling iron, Ashe, not agin you. I'll take my chances wi' the law.'

'I'm the only law you'll be meeting this side of hell, boy,' Ashe said remorselessly. 'Ain't got time for any other.' The Colt Lightning appeared in his hand. His tawny eyes showed no expression as it exploded twice and Clay screamed as the bullets emerged from his back trailing streams of grey lung and white bone fragments wrapped in a spray of red.

He danced backwards on buckling legs, twisted and fell on to the fire sending the coffee pot flying and spilling its steaming contents into the earth. His own blood was enough to douse the flames and put out the fire.

Ashe reholstered his gun, crossed to where two horses were hobbled and after finding the stolen money, set the animals free and returned into the lifting mist.

The rhythmic beating of the drums throbbed in Constance's brain. Bound upright to a thick stake by ankles and wrists she was forced to face the horrors of reality. Across the dancing, crackling flames of a small fire the dead eyes of Hank Jackson reflected the flames. Hank had been the driver of the wagon, a dour, taciturn man. He had died in terrible agony. The Indians had cut off his genitals and stuffed them into his screaming mouth. She closed her eyes to try and blot out the terrible reminder of the awful death that awaited them all, but that brought forth the memories of the event.

She could not remember how long ago it was that the Skinners had taken their money and ridden off leaving them alone in the desert. Two, maybe three days. The Indians had come soon after led by a huge, scarred Indian who Constance soon learned was the infamous Scar.

The Indians had toyed with them. Laughed and jeered when her father had offered the hand of friendship. Taunted them and finally this. Grown tired of their games they had taken the wagon party to their camp in the distant foothills and lashed them to stakes in the centre of a small, blind canyon. Beyond the mouth of the canyon lay the main camp of cone-shaped tepees. Darkness had long since fallen and beyond the dead man she could see the fires of the main camp separated from them by a well of darkness.

There were five left alive to wonder their fate, bound to stakes, three either side of the fire. Next to the dead Hank, her father, stripped to the waist, pale upper body red and blistered by the sun, groaned and shifted his head from side to side. Next to him the thin, bearded form of Professor Boyde. Though she had only known him a few days she had come to like the American professor. On either side of her were ranged Boyde's two sons. Frank, the older by two years over Michael.

Burial Ground 55

Both were dark haired and dark eyed, Frank the taller of the two. There had been friendly rivalry between the two boys over who would sit next to her. As each refused to give way to the other, she had found herself to be the filling in a pie so to speak, and had quite enjoyed the attention. Both boys now bore the marks of the Indians' attention. Stripped to the waist, as indeed she was, their young, hairless chests were caked and veined with dry blood from a dozen or more knife cuts. The knife cuts were nothing, not meant to maim or kill, just to bring the flies to add torment to their misery. The embarrassment of her own nudity had soon evaporated at the harsh treatment the Indians callously meted out. Only humiliation remained as braves, old and young came along, laughing and jeering, fondling her. Some had lifted her skirts, but with her ankles lashed together they were prevented their desires, for the time being, that was. She knew that she was living on borrowed time. Even now in the main camp the Indians were preparing for something. Feasting and getting drunk on whiskey. She could hear their shouts and laughter floating through the darkness mingled with the throbbing pulse of the drums.

An Indian lurched into view on the edge of the firelight clutching a bottle in one hand and weaving unsteadily on bowed legs. Her heart chilled as she recognized the man as their guard; a particularly vicious pig of a man who liked nothing better than to cause pain. He laughed and pointed as he passed the dead man and came to a pause before her father. She could not see what he was doing, but suddenly her father cried out in agony.

'Leave him alone!' Silas Boyde spoke up hoarsely, his normally strong voice made thin and hollow by their ordeal. For his interference the Indian turned his attention on him, slapping his head back and forth. Her father's cries had ceased as he now sagged unconscious in his bonds.

The Indian moved around behind Boyde and the firelight fell across his round, bland face with its single good eye. The other was a grey, blind thing. Sweat erupted over Boyde's face. There was a snapping sound as the Indian broke the bone in the little finger of Boyde's right hand. Boyde cried out, writhing against his bonds. The Indian jeered and laughed and drank from the bottle moving around the fire to stand swaying before Frank Boyde. The young man bit his lip and waited silently. This amused the one-eyed Indian even more. With a calloused palm he began to massage Frank's chest, painfully opening the scabbed-over cuts until blood flowed. He then gathered up a handful of alkali dust from the ground and began rubbing it into Frank's chest. The salt going into his open wounds sent waves of agony spearing through his chest. Frank cried out, unable to stop himself as the awful pain took a hold.

Laughing happily the Indian moved to Constance and leered darkly at her. Constance felt her insides crawl. The Indian drained the bottle and tossed it away into the darkness. She heard it smash with a musical tinkle as his hard hands began to rove over her breasts, digging roughly into the sunburned flesh. He sucked her nipples into hardness, squeezing and kneading even harder, filling her mind and body with pain. The cries that bubbled from her lips became screams of agony that only made the Indian laugh louder.

'Leave her alone, dog-shit Indian,' Michael shouted, unable to stand her screams any longer.

The smile left the Indian's face. He knew enough of the white man's tongue to know the youth had insulted him. He moved from Constance to Michael and the knife that suddenly appeared in the Indian's hand drove the pain from her mind.

'Me not dog shit,' the Indian rasped throatily. 'You die like him.' He jerked a thumb at the dead man and smiled as he tugged open the belt of Michael's pants and dragged them to his ankles. He pulled down the youngster's longjohns and stared with contempt at the boy's genitals.

'Please he didn't mean it,' Constance begged. For his part Michael was too terrified to be embarrassed.

'Cut balls off,' the Indian crooned and moved around the terrified youngster. 'White boy dog shit,' he grunted.

No one was prepared for what happened next, least of all the one-eyed Indian. The Indian was aware of a dark shape rising from the ground, seen from the corner of his good eye. A powerful hand was placed over his mouth and he was pulled back against a hard body. Something smooth and cold was drawn across his throat and hot blood splashed down his chest and ran chokingly into his lungs. He staggered forward as he was released, choking and gurgling, blood jetting darkly from his gaping lips and a neatly cut throat. As Constance watched with bulging eyes the man fell to his knees clutching at his leaking throat with red hands. As he toppled face down into the dust a figure moved into view.

'Ashe!' The name was torn from her lips in disbelief.

'Ma'am.' Ashe crouched and cut the ropes binding her feet with the bloody knife. He straightened and cut her wrists free and she toppled forward into his arms, clinging tightly and uttering his name over and over again. He gently broke her grip, slipped off his coat and draped it about her bare shoulders then swiftly set about freeing the others.

'My God, sir, I don't know how to thank you,' the professor, recovered from his faint, spoke in a dry, rasping voice. 'I thought we were dead for certain.'

'Ain't out of trouble yet, Professor,' Ashe pointed out.

'Silas, this is Ashe, the man I was telling you about,' the professor squeaked on. 'Professor Silas Boyde and his two sons, Frank and Michael.'

As they gathered around Ashe, he said, 'I'm right pleased to meet you folks, but there ain't time for introductions.'

'Someone's coming,' Michael Boyde whispered urgently.

'Back to your posts an' stand there like you're still

tied,' Ashe instructed. Before melting into the darkness he pulled his jacket from Constance. 'Sorry, ma'am,' he apologized, but Constance did not mind. Ashe dragged the body of the dead Indian away into the darkness as everyone waited.

Constance's heart was beating rapidly as the two braves, young bucks, staggered into view laughing and talking. The way they headed straight for her made no secret of their intentions.

She remained still as they closed in, pointing at her and laughing. The smell of whiskey issued from the two and it was doubtful if either realized what was happening to them as seconds later they lay writhing on the ground, their lives ebbing away in the growing pools of blood they lay in. Ashe had been swift and deadly and Constance could not suppress a shudder at the easy way death was handed out.

Ashe handed her back his coat then led them into the shadows where behind a rock he had a cache of weapons and a full water skin. After they had drunk their fill, Frank and Michael Boyde crowded round eagerly as Ashe handed out a shotgun and a Winchester. He had two handguns that he had taken from the Skinners. He handed one to Constance. She took it gingerly and Frank came across to explain how it worked. Her father put up his hands and backed away.

'I have no experience with guns, Ashe.'

'You'll be needing it afore we get out of here, Professor.'

'I'll take it, Mr Ashe.' Professor Boyde stepped

forward. 'I still have one good hand. I'll look after George here.'

'Just Ashe,' Ashe replied, handing the weapon to the man.

'How do you intend getting us out of here?' the professor asked.

'The Indians have corralled their mustangs near to the mouth of the canyon. We take what we need then stampede the rest and ride straight through Scar and his men.'

'And that is the only way?' the professor squeaked worriedly.

'The only way,' Ashe agreed. 'It means riding bareback I'm afraid.'

'Guns, horses with no saddles. Dear God, Ashe, it gets worse,' the professor cried.

'No, Professor. The worse is dying like that fella.' Ashe jerked his head in the direction of the dead Hank, and the professor swallowed.

'There must be an easier way. How did you get here?'

'By rope.' Ashe indicated into the darkness at the rear of the canyon. 'But afore you go getting your hopes up, the last thirty foot of the climb is sheer cliff an' a whole lotta praying 'cause the rope is that much short. I doubt any of you folks are in condition to take on a further seventy foot of hauling yourselves up a rope. And even if by some miracle you made it you'd end up stranded in the desert with no food, water or horses and be easy prey for the Indians. The only way is through the front gate. Just depends how much store you set by living.'

'A whole heap thanks, Ashe,' Frank said. 'I'm with you.'

'And me,' Michael said.

'You won't need to do a thing, Professor. Just climb on and take a good hold. Shut your eyes if'n you like. Once those mustangs start to run yours'll follow.' Ashe allowed himself a smile. 'I ain't come this far to leave you now, Professor.'

Constance moved to her father's side and put an arm about his naked shoulders.

'You can make it, Dad.'

The professor looked at her and his head bobbed.

'I'll try,' he agreed.

'Good, man,' Ashe applauded. 'Now, we uns have got a coupla things going for us. Scar and his boys are not expecting you to come riding outa here on the tail of a stampede. Secondly, they are so liquored up that when they do realize it we'll be long gone. Now the mustangs are gonna swing to the east outa the canyon being as that's the only clear path they got with the fire being straight ahead and the tepees to the west. Well that's good. To the east are a range of hills and a trail through them leads out into the big valley. My horse is stashed a coupla miles north. Once we reach him you'll have food and water. Any questions?' His eyes slid around the group, but no one said anything. He bent and retrieved a shoulder bag, settling it in position. 'Then let's go!'

Ashe led the party down to where the mustangs

milled nervously behind a crude wooden corral. Ashe slid between the horizontals and the others followed. The mustangs bunched and whickered, but Ashe soothed them. Soon he had six cut out and the party mounted. The professor was sprawled forward on his mustang's neck, arms wrapped tightly about its throat. Ashe just hoped he didn't strangle the poor beast.

Ashe undid the gate and reflected that life was just about to get interesting.

FIVE

The Indians were seated, or for the most part, sprawled around a single, big fire. They felt safe and content as they swallowed the white man's firewater. Black Dog felt the same as he threw up the white man's firewater and chunks of partially digested rabbit in the mouth of the canyon. He loved whiskey, but it always had this effect on him. He sank to his knees as his stomach continued to heave. Above the pounding of the drums and the pounding in his skull was a low rumble. He sank back on his calves. Behind him a half moon had pushed itself above the high rim-rock. Silver flooded past him, but such was the angle of the rising moon that it failed to penetrate far into the canyon. It was a sea of blackness lit at the far end by the orange glow of a fire.

As he stared towards the distant glow, it suddenly vanished behind a mass that had no size or shape. The rumble had grown louder and as he looked the first of the mustangs appeared in the moonlight. He stared, mesmerized as a solid wall of horse flesh, hooves pounding, manes flying, bore down on him. By the time he realized the danger he was in it was too late. He threw up his arms in a futile effort to ward off the advancing herd and seconds later disappeared beneath the thundering hooves, screams cut off abruptly as he was pulped into the ground.

The more sober of the Indians were on their feet as the herd galloped into view and swung east to avoid the fire. Scar saw a single rider break from the herd and charge towards the fire. He was reaching for his rifle when the boom of a shotgun filled the night air. Two Indians were lifted into the air and thrown back by the blast, chests and faces red ruins. The fire separated Scar from the rider and it was only when the rider slowed the mustang and dragged its head around, did he recognize him.

'Ashe!' The name was torn from Scar's lips as Ashe threw something into the fire. A few seconds later Scar knew what.

Dynamite!

The fire blew apart with a multiple roar, sending the Indians who were on their feet to the ground. Scar included. Braves leapt screaming to their feet as hot, glowing brands and ash rained down on them. One man, his head a mass of flames, ran screaming, trying to beat out the flames with his bare hands as the skin shrivelled on his face. His erratic movements took him on a collision course with a tepee; the hair and hide structure burst into flames. Other tepees, hit by the flying brands were already alight. Scar came to his feet as great billows

Burial Ground

of smoke drifted across the village adding confusion to the general panic.

Ashe caught up with the herd as it entered the hills, behind him over half the Indian camp was ablaze. He rode in the blinding wake of dust kicked up by the unshod hooves bringing his mount to a halt at the entrance of a narrow, high-walled defile that cut through the hills. Here the walls rose sheer to a height of forty feet. Slipping from his mustang he made himself busy as the thunder of hooves diminished ahead.

From the shoulder bag he wore he brought out two bundles of dynamite, four sticks to each, their fuses twisted together around a central length of fuse. He quickly found suitable crevices on either side to thrust the bundles into, then after lighting each fuse he leapt astride the mustang and kicked rib. The animal shot forward, neck stretched and had reached the far end of the defile when two thunderous explosions rent the air, their echoes chasing man and beast out into the wide valley. The force of the explosions sent tons of rock tumbling down on to the trail, blocking it.

Ashe kept the mustang going and caught up with the wagon party some ten minutes later. They had come to a halt while the rest of the herd had gone on, disappearing from sight and sound.

'Couldn't stop 'em, Ashe, they just kept running,' Frank said apologetically, kneeing his mount forward.

'Don't make no matter, son. It means Scar and his braves are on foot for awhile an' that gives us a chance to get outa here.' He glanced to where the professor now stood rubbing his sides and a smile appeared on his face. 'You done real well, Professor. We'll make a cowboy outa you yet.'

Professor Little rolled his eyes.

'God forbid,' he said fervently.

'Well mount up, folks, we've a piece to go afore we can rest up.'

A series of groans followed his words, but everyone climbed astride their mounts, even the professor, and Ashe led them away across the moon-silvered plain at the brisk trot into a series of foothills that lay at the base of the high ridge on the eastern edge of the valley. But the elation of escaping from the Indians was short lived. When they reached the place where Ashe had stashed the Morgan and the pack-mule, both were gone.

'Perhaps they wandered off,' the professor suggested, and Ashe shook his head as he studied the moon-silvered sand. In the churned up ground there were many prints. As the others slid wearily from their mounts, Ashe followed the tracks until they disappeared into deep shadow.

'What's happened, Ashe?' Boyde asked as Ashe returned to them.

'My horse and the pack-mule with all the food and water were led outa here by two or three men on horseback; white men,' he said grimly.

'How can you be sure it's white men and not Indians?' Michael asked.

'The horse thieves rode shod horses. Musta seen me leave. Damn!' Ashe turned away angry with himself. He must be geting old. If anyone had been watching him he should have known about it. He felt a touch on his arm and turned to find Constance at his side.

'It's not your fault, Ashe. You saved our lives and for that we are grateful.'

'Without food and water they won't be saved for long,' Ashe replied sourly.

'What do we do now?' the professor asked.

'Rest up an' at first light go looking for 'em. Tracks should be easy to follow.'

After a cold, uncomfortable night Ashe's words proved true. The tracks were easy to follow, a little too easy, The thieves had made no effort to hide them. Danger bells rang in Ashe's mind but, he chose to ignore them as they rode deeper and higher into the hills. It was only the ratchet clicking of lever mechanisms working bullets into breeches that made Ashe aware of the danger, but by then it was too late.

'Rest up a spell, folks,' a voice called from above. 'An' don' make no sudden moves lessen you wanna die.'

They were passing through a narrow ravine, Ashe in the lead, when the mocking voice came. Ashe snapped his head up. A man stood on the rocks above to the right of the trail, a tall, wild-bearded man in dirty, torn buckskin pants and coat. He held a Winchester in his big hands, Smith and Wesson .44 hitched high on his left hip.

'Sure are a sorry looking bunch of pilgrims, Cole,' a second voice jeered, this time behind and to the left. Ashe jerked his head around and focused on a second man high on the rocks. He was a head shorter than his companion and stockier. His shabby range-clothes were partially covered by an ankle-length, brown duster coat open at the front. He held a shotgun ready, a Navy Colt on his right hip. Both men wore black, high-crowned stetsons. The second man lacked the tangle beard of the first, making do with a dark coating of stubble about his long, lower jaw. There was amusement in both of the men's eyes as they stared down at the six, all the men but Ashe shirtless and riding Indian mustangs.

'Female ain't so bad though.' A third voice came from directly ahead and Ashe focused his gaze on a slim, red-haired youth dressed in black, his flame coloured hair reaching almost to shoulder level. He wore a pair of black-handled Navy Colts, slung low. He stood in the centre of the trail, thumbs hooked nonchalantly behind a silver belt buckle. The smile on his slim, pale face did little to hide the cold, deadly evil that lurked in his watery blue eyes. He eyed Ashe. 'Well, well, Ashe. I said we'd meet agin after you an' that dumb sheriff chased me outa Redrock.'

'Shoulda killed you when I had the chance,' Ashe said flatly, remembering the day two months ago when Red Clayton had lost his two sidekicks trying to rob the Redrock bank.

'You sure tried Ashe.' He laughed. 'Cost me two good boys in Willy and Monk, hadda get mysel' new partners. Meet Cole and Jeb; now I kin pay you back. Lose the iron, folks, an' do it real careful, double careful for you, Ashe.'

They could do little but obey and once they were disarmed Red Clayton waved them on into a small clearing decorated with a stand of scruboak on one side. There was a log cabin on the other side backing on to a wall of rock and between the two, the partially boarded entrance to a disused mine. Above the mine entrance a faded and split board bore the legend in red, 'Happy Days Mine'. Ashe guessed that it was an old gold mine. Near the cabin, the Morgan and pack-mule were hitched to a rail. The Morgan's head jerked and feet stamped as it saw Ashe. Ashe's face became hard.

'Why'd you take my animals?'

'Hell, you wouldn'ta come up here else,' Red cried. 'Off'n your horses folks, you is home.' By now the two others had joined Red. Both were grinning wolfishly, their eyes on Constance. 'You bin stirring up old Scar, Ashe, an' that sure don' settle well in my craw. Gotta nice little hideout here. Law an' soldier boys ain't too eager to come this far. Scar, he leaves us alone. We supply him with a few rifles now an' agin an' that ol' boy sure is tolerable good to we uns. Could change if'n he gets riled an' he's sure riled with you.'

'You allus did talk too much, Red,' Ashe broke in as he slid from his mustang and stood before the leader.

'Yeah, reckon I do at that,' Red agreed.

'I demand to know what the meaning of this is?' The professor stepped forward. Cole, the one with the beard, slammed the butt of his rifle into the professor's stomach sending the man to his knees.

'The meaning is, old man, you keep your face shut until you's spoken to.' The pair of Navy Colts appeared in Red's hands as Ashe took a threatening step forward. 'I won't kill you, Ashe, jus' blow your damn kneecaps off,' he said.

'Just what are you up to, Red?' Ashe demanded angrily.

'Makin' sure Scar knows who his friends are. Come on out, fella, he's all your'n.'

There was movement from the scrub oaks and Ashe's heart jumped as Wolf appeared, face split in an ugly grin as he approached Ashe.

'I take you to Scar,' Wolf grated and thumped his chest. 'I will be great warrior.'

Ashe stared at the red-headed outlaw.

'You bastard!' He spat the words and stepped forward heedless of Red's guns.

'Ashe, look out!'

He heard Constance scream out a warning as the shadow of the beardless man, Jeb, fell across him. He half turned and caught the jabbing butt of a shotgun just above the left ear. The world see-sawed for Ashe as he went to his knees, pain exploding through his head. His vision blurred and he fell helplessly forward on to the hot earth. Wolf dashed forward and delivered a couple of hard kicks to his ribs.

'You die soon, Ashe.' Wolf's gloating voice seemed to come from a long way off.

Ashe never completely lost consciousness. Through a welter of pain and sick dizziness, he was aware of his shirt being dragged from his body by the one called Cole, declaring that it was about time he had a new shirt. Jeb took his boots and hat and the two outlaws almost came to blows over his gunbelt. By the time he had recovered enough to take an interest in what was going on his hands had been bound behind his back and a rope halter tied around his neck. Hauled to his feet the end of the halter was given to Wolf sitting astride a piebald pinto.

'Have a safe journey, Ashe,' Red called mockingly as Wolf kicked the pony forward and jerked on the rope almost dragging Ashe off his feet.

Wolf was in jubilant mood as he rode down through the grey hills and out into the desert valley. Ashe was forced to keep pace or fall and be dragged. Without boots the sharp stones soon shredded the material of his socks and cut bloody lacerations in the soles of his feet.

'You kill Shoshoni, now Shoshoni kill you,' Wolf shouted over his shoulder. 'I become great warrior. Ride with Scar. Kill many white men.' He laughed at the thought.

Once clear of the hills the soft sand was kinder to Ashe's tortured feet. With heart pounding in his ears Ashe was forced to move at a trot, body glistening with sweat, mouth and throat as dry as the desert. The hot sun seared down mercilessly and the sand became red hot underfoot.

Time lost its meaning for Ashe. They were heading south and it seemed an eternity before Wolf called a halt and dropped the end of the halter. Ashe sank dizzily to his knees, heaving chest drawing air noisily into his burning lungs.

Wolf slid from the pinto and approached the bowed, kneeling figure, a grin stretching his lips. Using a foot he pushed Ashe on to his back then took a water skin from his shoulder. Ashe watched as the Indian pulled the leather plug from the water skin and poured water into his mouth. Some ran down his chin and splashed in gleaming beads on to his chest. Ashe felt as though his throat was filled with sand. His tongue felt swollen and bloated and threatened to choke him. He ran his leather-dry tongue over his parched, cracked lips.

Wolf stopped drinking and regarded Ashe with dark, taunting eyes.

'White man want drink?' He held out the water skin. Ashe scrambled on to his knees, holding his mouth towards the skin only to have it pulled away at the last minute by a laughing Wolf. It was only after three or four such tantalizing offers that Ashe realized he was following Wolf on his knees like some obedient puppy-dog. He sank back on his calves and Wolf laughed at his humiliation.

'Go to hell, red shit!' Ashe mumbled thickly.

'Soon meet Scar then white shit go to hell,' Wolf promised, laughed and turned his back on Ashe, moving towards the pinto. Ashe had been in situations before where there was nothing left to lose. In such situations, what the hell? Shaking the hair from his eyes he lurched to his feet. Adrenalin surged and he ran silently after Wolf.

Wolf was only aware of the other's presence at

the last minute. Not expecting to be attacked by a bound man he was caught off-guard. He was starting to turn when Ashe's shoulder caught him in the middle of the back.

Both men went down on to the sand. Ashe struggled to his feet first and as Wolf pushed himself up on straight arms the other's right foot made meaty contact under the Indian's chin. Ashe heard a crack and felt a stab of pain lance from his toes bringing a grimace to his face. Wolf was sent on to his back, but recovered in an instant, rolling aside and coming to his feet, knife appearing in his hand. A grin spread across Wolf's face, chasing the pain from his eyes. The initial surprise over, the odds had now turned in his favour.

'Mebbe cut you plen'y. Cut eyes out,' Wolf grated.

'Mebbe you'll just jaw me to death, Wolf. Never seen an Indian that liked to talk so much, lessen it was a yeller Indian,' Ashe taunted. He was past caring now. If Wolf killed him it would be a lot quicker than letting Scar do it.

Wolf dived for the end of the halter rope that lay in the sand between them. Ashe jumped backwards, jerking his head and Wolf's free hand missed the end of the rope. Ashe used a foot to pull the rope towards him out of the Indian's grasp. Wolf circled, knife gleamng in his hand.

'Wolf not kill you quick. Save you for Shoshoni death. Take a long time to die.'

'You shoulda been born a squaw, Wolf. Always gabbing an' never doing. Mebbe you are a squaw dressed in brave's clothes?' Ashe smiled as he goaded Wolf.

Wolf snarled, face dark with anger. He could not understand the white man, his defiance and aggression. He should have been begging for mercy yet he was not. It frightened Wolf. The Indian tried not to show his fear, yet his hesitancy in approaching the bound man spoke volumes of his unease.

'What's the matter, Wolf, can't do it on your own?'

The words stung Wolf. With a shrill, yipping cry he threw himself at Ashe. He wanted to hurt the white man, kill him, stop the words.

As Wolf bore down on him Ashe waited until the very last second before throwing himself down on his back, crushing his arms beneath him. Ignoring the pain he brought his feet up into Wolf's stomach, using the Indian's momentum to throw him over his head. Wolf cried out as he sailed through the air and crashed down heavily on his back in the sand the air exploding from his body.

As Wolf lay there winded, Ashe sat up and eased his bound hands beneath his buttocks in a desperate attempt to get his hands before him. He wriggled back, an eye on Wolf who was weakly attempting to rise. Ashe's hands were behind his knees as Wolf came groggily to his feet. Knees under his chin, Ashe rolled on his back as he tried to pull his feet through.

Wolf focused his eyes, shook his head and gave a growl. Gripping the knife tight he advanced on the rolled up man.

Heart thumping Ashe slid one foot through the

Burial Ground

circle of his bound arms and then the other. Wolf dived and Ashe rolled aside. Surprise registered in Wolf's face as he hit sand.

Ashe clambered to his feet and backed away, clawing the rope from his neck and using it as a whip as the Indian jumped up and charged. It flicked the Indian just below the left eye opening a cut. As Wolf came to a halt the rope whirled again and wrapped itself about the Indian's knife wrist. Ashe yanked and Wolf was jerked forward, knife flying from his grasp as he stumbled to his knees.

In a second Ashe was upon him. Getting himself behind the Indian he threw his bound wrists over the man's head and under his chin, pulling him back hard against his sweat running chest, the taut rope digging hard into Wolf's throat.

Wolf twisted and clawed at Ashe's wrists in a desperate effort to free himself. His nails ripped the flesh from Ashe's hands in bloody strands as he fought, but grimly Ashe held the stranglehold. Five minutes later Ashe let the lifeless body drop to the sand and fell weakly to his knees beside it breathing harshly. The effort had drained his strength dramatically. His arms felt like lead and it was several more minutes before he found energy to move.

Crawling to where the knife lay he sat back on his calves, gripped the knife between his knees and sawed at the bindings about his wrists. More precious time was lost, but finally the rope parted and he was free.

SIX

After Wolf had left with Ashe as his prisoner, Jeb Anders, the beardless outlaw, put Ashe's hat and boots on while Cole Meaken settled Ashe's gunbelt about his waist. He had won the battle over the gunbelt.

'Feels real swell,' Cole said. 'Gonna save me the shirt for best.'

'How do I look, Red, in my new hat an' boots?' Jeb called out.

'You both look real fine,' Red complimented with a smile.

'Hey, Red. What we gonna do with them folks?' Cole jabbed a dirty thumb in the direction of the cabin.

'I'm doing me some thinkin' on that problem, but I reckon what we uns got here is some hostages.'

Cole looked puzzled and fingered his bushy, tangled beard.

'What the hell kinda hoss is that?' he demanded finally.

'Ain't no kinda hoss. Hostages.'

'Ain't no kinda stage I ever come across,' Cole said with a frown and Red rolled his eyes.

'Hostages is folk you hold so that if'n the law comes after you, you tell 'um to back off 'cause if'n they don't you's gonna plug the hostages.'

Cole whipped his hat off and scratched his mop of hair.

'Ain't we gonna plug 'em anyway?'

'Sure we are,' Red agreed, 'but the law don' know that an' 'cause they don' know that, they gotta do as we say.'

'P'rhaps they's worth money?' Jeb spoke up. 'Heard tell of a gang over Denver way who grabbed this important guy an' then telled his family that if they didn't come up wi' a whole heap of cash they'd kill him for sure.'

'Tha's called kidnapping,' Red said knowledgeably.

'Figure them folks is worth money?' Cole looked interested.

'Mebbe,' Red replied cautiously. 'Get 'em out here an' we'll sure as hell find out.'

The five were marched from the cabin and lined up before Red with Cole and Jeb keeping each end of the line covered.

'This is an outrage,' Silas Boyde cried. 'I don't know what you boys are getting out of it, but one thing's for sure, it'll be big trouble for you.'

'How'd you make that out?' Red asked.

'We have government permission to be here. The army will be out looking for us.'

His words brought a smile to Cole's bearded

features.

'Ain't no soldier-boys coming out here, not wi' ol' Scar on the prod,' he called.

'An' that's the pure truth,' Jeb agreed.

Red made no comment, his eyes on Constance, tongue licking his thin lips. Constance reddened beneath his silent scrutiny and clutched the coat she wore closer to her body.

'You must be pretty important folks then?' he ventured, eyes remaining on Constance.

'Very, my good man.' The professor stepped between Constance and Red. 'You would be well advised to make sure nothing happens to us.'

'How come you speak so damned funny, sassy-mouth?' Red asked with a frown.

'I'm from England, here by invitation from your government.' The professor assumed his most pompous air. In the college halls of Oxford it was guaranteed to quell the most belligerent boy. It did nothing to these rough, unkempt outlaws.

'That's a powerful long way to come. Why? What's out here for you?'

'We are archaeologists on our way to study Spirit Canyon.' He looked into Red's blank face. 'We study the remains of ancient people to see how they lived.'

'Why?' Red asked. 'Seems a damn fool thing for a grown man to be doing.'

'It helps us to understand ourselves if we learn how our ancestors lived.'

'Dammit to hell if'n that ain't the queerest tale I ever done heard,' Jeb sang out.

'You figure to poke 'bout them ol' Injun bones an' tell us why we uns is here?' Cole called out, mystified.

'Not quite,' the professor began.

'Look, if it's money you want, get us back to civilization and I'll see you are well paid for your trouble.' Silas Boyde broke into the conversation.

'Now that's more like it,' Jeb said with a grin.

'You got money?' Red demanded.

'Not with me, but it can be arranged once we are safe.'

'How much?'

'Five thousand dollars.'

Red pursed his lips in a silent whistle.

'That's a heap of money,' he said.

'Get us to safety and it's yours,' Boyde promised.

'Sure is somethin' to think on,' Red said slowly.

'What's happened to Ashe?' Constance asked from behind her father.

Red moved the professor aside with a hand.

'Don' you go worrying your pretty head 'bout Ashe, ma'am. He's gone a-visiting with his Injun friends.' Red's words brought sniggers from Cole and Jeb.

'Reckon it could be a real long visit too.' Cole chuckled.

'When they redskins take a shine to a body, it sure is hard to get away,' Jeb threw in.

'Is it a deal?' Silas Boyde demanded of Red.

'I'll chew on it awhile,' Red replied. 'Put 'em in the mine, boys.'

'This is preposterous,' the professor fumed

indignantly.

'Jus' keeping you safe like you asked. Wouldn't want you folks running loose in the desert. Might get lost.' Red grinned. 'Now move out.' As he spoke Jeb was busy kicking the crumbling, wooden panels away from the mine entrance. 'But not you, girl.' He indicated Constance and broad, lecherous grins filled the faces of Cole and Jeb.

'Now wait a minute.' Frank stepped forward and the butt of Cole's rifle slammed hard against his left cheekbone, splitting skin and sending the young man to his knees.

'Watch yer mouth, boy,' Cole growled.

Red moved in on the hesitant Constance, grabbed her arm and dragged her out of the line.

'I must protest,' the professor cried and suddenly found himself looking down the barrel of a Navy Colt that had appeared in Red's free hand.

'You wanting to die that bad, old man?' he hissed. The facade of the simple, unimaginative outlaw giving way to a darker, deadlier being. He thumbed the hammer back and the blood drained from the professor's face. He saw only death in the merciless eyes of the outlaw.

'Please, she's my daughter,' he begged.

Red lifted the gun and rested the end of the barrel against the professor's forehead.

'Looks like she's 'bout to become an orphan,' Red whispered. There was no compassion in the outlaw's face, just the naked desire to kill.

'No!' Constance shrieked tearing herself free. 'I'll do whatever you want. Please don't hurt him.'

For a second it seemed as though the outlaw had not heard her words, then he lowered the gun letting the hammer down gently.

'Move out.'

This time there was no dissent. Michael hauled his dazed brother to his feet and supported him under one arm, following the others into the mine. The professor paused at the entrance.

'Please don't hurt her. I'll double the offer. Ten thousand dollars. Let her come with me,' he whimpered.

'Get inside, old man,' Red said roughly. 'Jeb's gonna be on guard outside. If'n anybody shows a face they's gonna get it blowed clean away.' He took Constance's arm again in a painful grip. 'Fact is both boys is gonna be on guard.' He pushed Constance towards the cabin and jerked his head for Cole to join Jeb. Cole grinned and said nothing.

Once in the cabin Red reholstered his gun and removed his gunbelt, tossing it on to a battered table. He was smiling wolfishly as he moved in on Constance. She backed away until the rear wall stopped her and once more clutched the coat to her body.

'What do you want?' her voice quavered.

'You know what I want, girl. Depends on how much you want your pa to stay alive?'

She looked at him with contemptuous eyes.

'You bastard,' she snarled, and his grin broadened.

'Reckon you could be right,' he agreed.

She made no move to stop him after that as he

stripped the clothing from her body and on the dusty, creaking boards of the cabin floor took her, driving himself roughly into her, mistaking her cries of pain for passion. Later, his lust spent, he pulled up his pants and buckled on his gunbelt. Before he swaggered from the cabin he said, 'Have to let Cole and Jeb take their turn with you later an' they ain't as refined as me.'

When he had gone tears welled in her eyes and trickled slowly down her cheeks. Naked, she dragged herself into a corner and wept.

It was almost noon by the time Ashe found himself back at the start of the trail into the hills that led to the outlaws' camp. He wore Wolf's calf-length, moccasin boots. The middle toe on his right foot was broken and the boot helped support it. He had also acquired Wolf's knife and Winchester. The latter had only two rounds in it and Wolf had no more shells on him. Shirtless and hatless Ashe rode the pinto as close as he dared and then went on foot. His feet were sore from the cuts that criss-crossed the soles, but the pain only served to heighten his awareness. Finally he clambered up and bellied over sun-baked rocks until he could look down into the tiny clearing before the cabin.

Red, Cole and Jeb sat in rickety chairs at the battered table that had been brought out from the cabin. They were laughing and talking, the words just a drone to Ashe's ears. He scanned the area with his tawny eyes. He could see nothing of the wagon party, but he noted that the mine had been opened up, giving him a good idea where they were, but not knowing if the mine was a prison or a grave.

'Hurry up wi' that food, girl,' Red bellowed, and Ashe looked as a figure moved within the shadow hung doorway of the cabin and emerged into the light of day.

Ashe's heart froze and then a murderous anger swept all traces of humanity from his eyes and set deep lines in his face, Naked, Constance carried plates of beans with chunks of bread to the men seated at the table. Even from here Ashe could see the humiliation and shame carved in the set of her face. Blood showed on the inside of her thighs and the rage that simmered within him threatened to boil over and send him leaping down regardless of his own safety.

Cole and Jeb jeered, shouted coarse insults and crude suggestions while their grimy hands fingered her body. Ashe kept the anger within him bottled. There would be a time to release it, but that time was not yet if he was to get the girl away. He needed to even the odds a little and the chance came some fifteen minutes later when Cole Meaken rose to his feet.

'Gonna take me a leak,' he announced, swaying a little, for between them they had drunk almost a bottle of whiskey.

'What yer telling us fer? Need someone to hold it?' Jeb brayed.

Cole said something then lurched towards the

rocks where Ashe lay and Ashe wriggled back out of sight. Cole disappeared from view. Ashe heard his boots scraping rock then the sound of urine hitting the ground. The outlaw belched and broke wind.

Ashe moved back and found a place to scramble down to the ground level, thankful for the silence of the soft-soled mocassins. Cole had his back to Ashe as he buttoned up his pants. The first and last time he was aware of Ashe's presence was when a hand clamped itself over his mouth and the blade of Wolf's knife slid between his ribs and sliced into his heart. Death was almost instantaneous. Ashe felt the man grow rigid with shock then he slumped and his legs buckled. Ashe lowered him to the ground and swiftly unbuckled his own gunbelt from the man's waist. Ashe felt a surge of savage elation as he settled the belt about his waist and quickly fastened the leg ties. After checking to make sure the weapon was loaded, he circled the rocks to come up with the cabin to his left and the seated men some fifteen feet straight ahead.

'Hey, Cole, what yer doing round there, playing wi' yourself?' Jeb sang out as Ashe positioned himself. The two were alone, Constance having returned to the cabin.

'He's too busy dying,' Ashe said bleakly and stepped into view. He held the Winchester waist high and as he spoke the weapon cracked out its message of death. The bullet caught Jeb, who was seated on the cabin side of the table, in the chest, throwing him, chair and all, backwards, blood gouting from a hole above his heart.

Red came to his feet, kicking his chair aside, as Ashe levered the last bullet into the breech and pulled the trigger. The hammer snapped on a dud round and an unholy smile jumped across Red's face.

'Now ain't that a shame,' he said sardonically, his hands hovering claw-like over the butts of his guns. 'Heard tell you're fast, Ashe, but I'm faster.'

'Only one way to find out,' Ashe replied grimly.

'That's a fact,' Red agreed and a scowl hardened his face. 'Hell, Ashe. That's another two partners you've done killed on me,' he said reproachfully.

'Shoulda chosen better.'

'I will next time.' Red was cool, unworried, confident of his own prowess. He shook his head. 'I knowed I shouldn't've trusted that damned Injun.'

'You can tell him that when you meet him in hell,' Ashe replied, and Red laughed.

'You got balls, Ashe, an' I surely do admire you for that, but time's a-wasting an' I've a hankering to be going down on that woman again. I'm gonna enjoy killing you.'

It was an enjoyment that the brash outlaw was never to fulfil, for that moment Constance appeared in the doorway of the cabin. She had pulled on her skirt, but her upper body was still bare, but it was not that made Ashe's eyes pop, it was the shotgun she held in her hands.

Red flicked a glance at the doorway, drawn there by Ashe's sudden surprise. Constance was the last person the outlaw saw. The shotgun roared, belching smoke and flame from both barrels.

The heavy shot at close range was devastating. It caught Red high on the right shoulder and neck. Red's head flew from his shoulders trailing strings of flesh and sinew. Like some gory fountain found only in the depths of hell, blood jetted high into the air from the neck stump. As his head left his body, the force of the shot spun the outlaw and his right arm fell from his shoulder.

Ashe watched in horrified fascination as the headless corpse toppled and crashed down into the dust. Its remaining limbs spasmed in dirt and then it lay still.

Constance remained standing there like some beautiful, deadly statue. Ashe moved across to her and gently took the still smoking weapon from her nerveless hands.

'He deserved to die.' Her voice was husky with emotion. 'He, he ...'

Her voice broke and she fell sobbing into Ashe's arms.

He dropped the shotgun and held her to him.

'You did right, ma'am. He was an animal. He's killed many a good man and the law's been after him for a long time.' He broke her hold gently and smiled down into her face. 'Where are the others?'

'In ... in the mine.' She forced a hesitant smile. 'You have a habit of turning up at the right time. How do you manage it?'

'Just a knack I guess. Get dressed. I'll get the others.'

'Ashe! Good God, man, we thought you were dead,' the professor cried after Ashe had called them from the mine.

'It's a mistake that's been made before,' Ashe brushed off the remark as they gathered, jubilantly, around him.

'Constance. Have you seen Constance?' The professor sounded concerned.

'I'm here, Father.' Constance appeared from the cabin and came towards them, Ashe's buckskin jacket around her shoulders.

The professor gave her a hug.

'Are you all right? Did they hurt you?'

She gave a wan smile.

'No, Dad, I'm fine. You look as if you could all do with some food?'

There were no dissenters.

Ashe threw her disappearing back an admiring look. She was one hell of a girl.

SEVEN

Perched on a ridge of rock that ran a north/south line, Ashe watched the Indians in the distant valley, strung out in a long, snaking column coming from the south. They were Shoshonis all right and he had no doubt in his mind that it was Scar and his braves. They had gathered their scattered mustangs and were now searching for him and the others.

Ashe cast an eye to his right and downwards where he could see members of the wagon party. He looked back towards the distant Indians, reflected thoughtfully, nodded and began clambering down from the ridge.

The group looked more human now. Before Ashe had rescued them from the Shoshonis, he had stopped by their wagon and collected a change of clothes for each and extra food. These he had left with the pack-mule. With the animal back in their posession they now had a chance to change their clothes. For Constance, petticoats and skirts were out for this wild, untamed piece of country. She now wore levi's and a shirt. His own clothes back, Ashe joined the others. The bodies of the three outlaws had been consigned earlier to the mine.

'See anything up there, Ashe?' the professor asked, peering owlishly at him.

'Too much,' Ashe said grimly. 'Scar and his braves are ten to fifteen miles south of here and heading this way. Be here in an hour or so.'

'Can we get back to the fort?' Boyde queried, and Ashe shook his head.

'You gentlemen are going to get your wish. The only way out of here is north, through Spirit Canyon. If'n we can get to the canyon then we stand a chance. The Indians won't follow us in. To them it's a bad place.'

'Well that is to our advantage, surely?' the professor said.

'Mebbe.' Ashe gave a bleak smile. 'The only advantage is that the canyon will be the nearest water supply after we leave here and we'll be needing it. The quickest way to the canyon is across the salt desert and even Scar won't risk that, not if'n he's got a lick o' sense.'

'What's this desert like?' the professor asked curiously.

'You'll find that out for yourself soon enough, Professor. Time for jawing ain't now. We need to be on the move pronto!'

In the afternoon sun the huge, alkali plain that Ashe called the salt desert, shone with the glaring whiteness of a vast, flat snowfield, cracked like the surface of a badly glazed, china plate.

Where the six riders had stopped their horses to view the awesome sight, the grey flanks of the craggy hills that surrounded them flowed into the whiteness and disappeared. All that was left was the flat, baking salt plain spreading in all directions for as far as the eye could see. The two professors and Constance rode the dead outlaws' saddled horses while the Boyde brothers continued with their saddleless mustangs. Ashe still wore the moccasin boots while his feet mended, his own boots stuffed in his saddle-bags.

'It looks awfully big,' Constance said nervously.

'Can we make it across, Ashe?' Silas Boyde asked.

'We've got water and the horses are fresh,' Ashe countered.

'How long will the crossing take?' the professor asked.

'Two days if'n we're lucky.'

'What if we are not lucky?'

Ashe afforded himself a bleak smile.

'Then we'll be dead,' came the blunt reply.

Boyde gave a nervous chuckle.

'You don't pull your punches, Ashe.'

'Call it as I see it, Silas,' Ashe replied. The American professor insisted that he call him Silas. 'Nothing lives out there an' that makes it all the harder for living things to stay alive. It's dryer than hell on a hot day, but with Scar smoking our tails I'd sooner take my chances with the desert.'

'Point taken,' Silas Boyde said.

Ashe reached into his saddle-bag and pulled out a small, brass-cased, army compass and commenced to study the needle as it slowly settled. Once they left the safety of the hills the compass would be the only thing between them and death. In the heart of the featureless salt flats it was only too easy to wander in a circle until the water ran out and death stepped in. He slipped the compass into the breast pocket of his shirt, tipped his hat forward and said, 'Let's go!'

It was some two hours later that Scar and his braves rode into the outlaws' camp. They had found Wolf where Ashe had left him and it wasn't long before they discovered the bodies of the dead outlaws in the mine. Scar sent out scouts and it was almost another hour before he received news.

'Six riders, one pack-mule enter white desert,' Running Bear said.

'How long?' Scar asked.

'The sun was there in the sky.' Running Bear pointed up and Scar nodded. Running Bear had seen the passing of many summers. Age had carved deep lines into his nut-brown face. Scar trusted the old man's word. Running Bear could read signs that others could not see. Scar motioned to four braves. He spoke briefly to them, then under Running Bear's leadership, they rode away.

Scar led the rest of his braves in the same direction, but at a more leisurely pace. They finally came to the place where Ashe had led his party into the flats and in the hills made camp. Later, standing alone on the edge of the flats he looked out over the baking whiteness. If all went according to plan the hated whites would be forced to return and he would be waiting for them.

Day gave way to night and it wasn't until dawn flushed the eastern horizon that Running Bear and the four returned. Scar was awake to greet them.

'All went well, Running Bear?'

Running Bear's leathery face broke in a grin.

'It is done as you said.'

Scar nodded in satisfaction.

'Then they will have to return.' He smiled. 'You have done well. Rest now.'

Scar moved to a rocky knoll on the edge of the camp and gazed out across the white wilderness that spread like a grey ghost away from the hills in the brightening, morning light. Still cool from the night's embrace, soon it would bake beneath the cruel gaze of the sun and they would return.

Ashe jerked awake, sitting up and dragging the blanket about his shoulders as the night chill penetrated his body and joints. He had not meant to fall asleep, but tiredness had finally claimed him in the early hours of the morning. He rose to his feet still clutching the blanket about him.

The fire that they had huddled about when darkness had fallen had long since burnt itself to a pile of grey, shadowy ash. To the east the first light of day was beginning to spread. He knew that soon the chill of the night would be a distant memory as the sun rose.

He looked at the others huddled in a circle about the dead fire, faint snores coming from the professor. The animals, hobbled to the right lifted their heads as he came to his feet and the Morgan whickered. They had brought a bundle of dry scrub on the pack-mule and as Ashe went to the bundle the others began to stir.

Constance raised herself up. 'Is it always this cold?'

Ashe smiled as he piled the faggots.

'You won't be saying that in an hour's time.'

The light coming across the vast, cracked plain was rapidly growing. It was Frank Boyde who made the discovery. He had gone to where their water skins were piled to get water for coffee. His shout brought them all running. As they gathered around he wordlessly held out one of the water skins to Ashe. Where yesterday it had been fat with water, now it was empty, slit open by a sharp knife and the precious water gone. It was the same story with the eleven other water skins.

'How could this happen?' the professor cried in dismay.

'Scar!' Ashe replied grimly.

'You said he wouldn't follow us.'

'He won't. He's just going to sit there and wait for us to return.'

'I don't understand, Ashe?' Silas Boyde cut in.

'I underestimated Scar. He sent a few braves out to follow us and wait until we camped for the night.

They waited until we were asleep then crept in, cut open the skins and then hightailed it back to Scar.'

'It could have been our throats,' Constance said shocked.

'Scar is playing a deeper game,' Ashe replied. 'He likes to play games. A sneak attack in the night would not have the value of having us crawl outa this hell-land and into his waiting arms.'

'How'd you mean, Ashe?'Michael Boyde asked.

'Without water it would be suicide to continue on. We could easily get back to where we started, but Scar would be waiting and that's what he's hoping on, us to come crawling back. Sorry, folks, my fault, shoulda stayed awake.'

'Nonsense,' the professor said staunchly as he wiped dust from his spectacles vigorously. 'We are all to blame. We should have worked something out instead of leaving it all up to you.'

'He's right, Ashe,' Silas agreed quickly. 'There's no blame that we can attach to you that we can't attach to ourselves. You've saved our lives twice already.'

There were murmurs of agreement all round.

'We've also got our own canteens that we kept by us during the night. I know mine is full,' the professor spoke up.

'Mine too, Dad,' Constance said. 'Mike, Frank?' The Boyde brothers nodded.

'Same with me,' Silas cried. 'We do have water.'

'But not enough,' Ashe broke in, hating to dampen their growing euphoria.

'I say we go on,' the professor said and his words were followed by a chorus of all round agreement.

'You don't understand,' Ashe began, but the professor interrupted him, raising a hand.

'But we do, Ashe. The prospect of what would happen to us should we fall into Scar's hands is far more terrifying than anything this salt flat can offer. Will you still lead us, Ashe?' Five pairs of eyes focused on Ashe and waited expectantly.

Ashe looked from one to the other and a smile twitched his lips.

'Can't fault you folks on guts, brains mebbe.' He bobbed his head. 'Sure I'll lead you.'

'And I'm sure we'll make it.' The professor beamed. 'Now how about breakfast before the sun gets too hot?'

Beneath the midday sun that burned down pitilessly from a deep azure sky, the salt flats threw back heat and glare causing the strung out group to squint through barely open eyes. The sun sucked the moisture from their bodies and spirit from their souls. Ashe's tongue felt like a piece of old, dry leather in his mouth that was trying to choke him. He desperately wanted to drink deep and long from the canteen; slake the thirst that filled his throat with cottonwool and cracked the flesh on his dry lips, but he forced the craving aside. Survival meant rationing the water, the pitifully small amount they each carried and had to share with their horses.

He reflected dully that it was a mad idea. They should have gone back, fought it out with Scar.

Probably died in the attempt, but a bullet would have been far better than a lingering death by thirst.

A hot wind fanned across the barren salt flats raising a distance haze, hiding the low, purple mountain ridge that showed on all horizons and it was only by constant use of the compass that Ashe kept them on course as they travelled mile after mile across the heat shimmering plain.

They were given a grim reminder of their own fragile mortality when at one point they passed the remains of a wagon, the bones of its two horses still wrapped in the traces where they had fallen. The canvas top hung in tatters from the wooden spars. The wagon was canted at an angle where a wheel had broken from the axle. The skeletons of its five occupants lay amid the crumbling remains of their personal possessions. Ragged, shadow-haunted eye sockets watched their passing and gaping jaw bones laughed in silent mockery.

It was mid-afternoon when the professor's horse stumbled to its knees, pitching the small man on to the hard, cracked ground. The professor managed to rise groggily to his feet, the horse could not. Foam decorated its muzzle and its flanks heaved. It tried to rise, but the effort was too much. It rolled on its side and lay twitching, eyes rolling. Ashe slid wearily from the Morgan and approached the stricken beast. The animal was dying: all he could do was put it out of its misery He reached for his Colt Lightning.

They continued their journey, the professor

riding double with Silas Boyde. It was an hour later that they came upon the fish-like fin of rock rising defiantly from the salt plain. Ashe led them towards it and into the thankful shade it provided. It was still hot, but at least it was out of the sun.

'We'll rest up here for a while,' Ashe rasped dryly.

As the sun reddened the western horizon, Scar paced back and forth along the edge of the salt flats. He had expected Ashe and those with him to have returned by now. He had sent scouts out to look for them and now paced as he waited for them to return.

Deep shadows were filling the wells between the hills with purple as Running Bear returned.

'Well?' Scar barked impatiently.

'They have gone on into the white desert,' Running Bear said.

Scar peered out across the greying whiteness, eyes lidded.

'Then let the desert take them.'

With the coming of night and a sickle moon to cast a pale ghostly glow over the white, salt plain, Ashe led the group out.

'We'll travel by night,' he had said to the tired group. 'It may be our only hope if'n we reckon to come out of this alive.' Wrapped in his poncho against the night chill, the others using their blankets, they managed to maintain a brisk pace. Tired, weary, thirsty and hungry, by the time dawn came they were ready to drop, but Ashe refused to let them rest.

'How much further, Ashe?' the professor asked in a croaking voice, as the sun rose to replace the chill with a blistering heat.

'Half a day, mebbe a little longer.' Ashe shrugged, not willing to commit himself.

Exhausted they continued at a slower pace, the heat goading and tormenting them. By mid-morning Constance's horse had fallen and she rode double with Ashe. Midday saw the mustang that Frank Boyde rode drop dead beneath him. To make matters worse, a wind that seemed to blow from the very jaws of hell itself, wrapped them in a cocoon of swirling, bitter alkali dust that clawed into their eyes and nostrils. Ashe made them all dismount, tie bandannas about their lower faces and lead their animals. He knew they were living on borrowed time. Their water was gone and unless they reached the other side of the salt flats soon their chances of survival were very slim. Ashe referred constantly to the compass to keep them on course in the choking dust.

Time lost its meaning, but it was some time during the afternoon that the ground underfoot began to change. Subtle at first, so that none realized it; slabs of rock began to snag at their dragging feet, then clumps of tough, wiry brown grass. The dust thinned and then cleared dramatically and half a mile ahead brush scattered hills heaved themselves from the salt and rolled towards high, red, flat topped buttes.

'Ashe, we've made it,' the professor shouted hoarsely, pulling the bandanna from his face. Caked white from head to toe, the area where the bandanna had been showed pink. Slapping dust from his clothes Ashe grinned inanely.

'Sure looks that way,' he agreed.

Everyone forgot their tiredness and thirst, jumping about and laughing as the sight brought forth renewed energy. The professor insisted on shaking everyone's hand.

A mile into the hills as grass began to thicken underfoot, they came upon a stream, gurgling and chuckling out its welcome to them. The group, even the professor, forgot everything and threw themselves into the shallow stream, rolling and splashing, letting the cool water soak into clothes and flesh. Ashe, showing more restraint, led the animals, one by one to drink, careful they did not drink too much to begin with. It was only after they had been taken care of and were cropping at the grass did he attend to himself, following the others' example.

Later he climbed to the top of a hill and called the others up. When they joined him they found themselves looking down on to a vast, sandy plain peppered with weather eroded buttes. To the east and west high, gaunt grey cliffs clawed at the blue sky with sharp, splintered crags. Directly ahead, some five or six miles beyond the buttes, rose a massive buttress of red sandstone that formed a forbidding red wall stretching from east to west. At one point, clearly visible in the red folds, the wall had been split as though a giant axe had cleaved the rock. Ashe pointed.

'Spirit Canyon, folks.' He let them absorb the news before continuing. 'We'll make camp by the stream and rest up for the rest of the day. Tomorrow we'll head for the canyon. Once through we'll be within two days' ride of the Humboldt River and safety.'

'What about Scar?' Silas Boyde asked. 'Will he follow us?'

'Not across the salt flats. If he does decide to circle the salt flats, it'll take him mebbe three, four days to get here and by that time we'll be long gone. More'n likely he figures us for dead anyway an' won't bother.'

The meal that evening of beans and jerky was further supplemented by Ashe shooting a couple of rabbits. By the time they rolled into their blankets, the ordeal of the trek had become a dark, fading memory.

Exhausted as they were, Ashe insisited on a rota of night watches. They were still in hostile territory and this time he was leaving nothing to chance.

EIGHT

The old man, arms folded across his skinny chest, stood obstinately in their path. He was flanked on either side by a young, sullen-faced buck, bare chested and bare legged. They carried long-shafted throwing spears decorated with eagle feathers just below the head while at their slim waists hung knife and tomahawk. The old man's face was as lined and seamed as the massive red cliff that loomed behind him. Ashe reined the Morgan to a halt, a shotgun cradled casually in the crook of his left arm.

'Shoshoni land. White man not welcome,' the old man intoned in a reedy voice. He was clad in decorated buckskin and wore a brown derby sporting a single feather on his head with thin streamers of white hair tumbling wispily from beneath the brim. Ashe wondered what poor devil had lost his hair in exchange for the hat.

'We come in peace, old man, not war. We wish only to pass through the canyon,' Ashe said.

The old man's dark eyes swept scornfully over them. As before Constance rode with Ashe. The professor and Silas shared a second horse, and Frank Boyde sat astride the mustang. The load from the pack-mule had been distributed amongst the horses, allowing Michael Boyde to ride the mule. A smile passed fleetingly across the old man's weathered-carved face. Ashe guessed that they must look a pretty rag-tag bunch.

'Spirit Canyon sacred. Once Shoshoni burial ground. Not for white man.'

Ashe fixed him with cold, tawny eyes.

'We mean no disrespect to your ancestors, old man, but we're fixing to ride through whether you like it or not.' He hardened his tone and let the shotgun drift until it pointed at the veteran. The old man eyed Ashe without flinching.

'You wear dead Shoshoni moccasins,' he accused flatly.

'Figured he wouldn't be needing 'em again,' Ashe replied. 'You're wearing a dead white man's hat.'

'Figured he would not need,' the old man mocked and grinned. Ashe stared bleakly at him and the smile faded. 'Spirit Canyon is only for the dead.'

'An' you could be joining 'em real soon if'n you try and stop us.'

'Ashe, I must protest.' The professor slid from his shared horse and approached the old man, appalled at Ashe's truculent approach. 'We do not wish to harm you or violate ancient customs. All we seek is permission to pass through the canyon.'

'I've got the permission in my hand,' Ashe

pointed out mildly, earning himself a furious glare from the professor. The professor's attempt at authority was not helped that after losing his own hat he now wore one of the outlaws'. It was a little on the large size and gave him a comical appearance.

The old man stared at Ashe.

'Grey Dog is old and with age comes wisdom.' His eyes drifted back to the professor after resting, for an instant, on the shotgun. 'I cannot stop you from entering Spirit Canyon, glass eyes.' He referred to the professor's spectacles. 'It is bad place. Shoshoni find new burial ground. Demons now dwell in canyon. Live in the House of Bones.'

'Then what are you doing here, old man?' Ashe asked.

'I make medicine. Keep demons away from new burial ground,' came the matter-of-fact reply as though it was nothing unusual.

'Well one got away. Calls himself Scar,' Ashe said.

A look of contempt crossed the old man's face.

'Scar bad Shoshoni. Bring much trouble to Indians.'

'Well he's sure given me some grief, so stand aside, old man.'

Grey Dog, the old man, eyed Ashe for a long second then moved aside.

'You never leave Spirit Canyon. The Demons from the House of Bones will not let you,' he said solemnly.

A thin smile tugged at Ashe's lips.

'Then I'll come back and haunt you. Mount up, Professor.'

The professor glared at Ashe a second time, but did as he was bid.

'When the rocks sing you will die,' Grey Dog called out darkly.

'I'll keep it in mind. Move out, folks.'

As they rode away from the three, Constance asked, 'What did he mean about the rocks singing and the House of Bones?'

'Beats me, ma'am. Just crazy Indian talk I guess, but all the same there's somethin' about that old boy that makes me itch.' He cast a look back over his shoulder and stiffened. The old man was alone, his young companions gone.

They rode on, the area about them becoming increasingly more rocky towards the canyon mouth. Ashe looked back again, Grey Dog was still there, arms folded watching them.

With his unease growing by the minute, Ashe waited until a cluster of rocks hid them from view, then leapt from the Morgan, tossing the reins to Constance.

'Ashe?'

'Keep going. I'll catch up,' he said with an urgency that stilled any questions. She nodded dumbly and kept the Morgan going. Those ahead had disappeared from view and saw nothing of this. Ashe pressed himself back into the rocks and waited. He didn't have long to wait.

Hidden from view from above by a small overhang, he heard stealthy, moccasined feet slap

Burial Ground 107

rock. One of the bucks who had been with the old man, jumped from the rock that Ashe sheltered beneath to a lower one ahead. He landed in a crouch and remained still, eyes scouting ahead.

Ashe had very little choice but to make his play. The group were still probably hidden by rocks, but once the Indian saw that Constance was alone, Ashe's element of surprise would be gone. He had hoped to have some indication of the second Indian's presence, but he could not wait.

'Looking for someone, fella?' Ashe stepped from his cover as he spoke.

The Indian spun on his toes, still crouching, eyes opening wide as he saw Ashe. He sprung to his feet, fury in his dark eyes. Oblivious to the shotgun Ashe carried he drew back the spear into a throwing position. The shotgun roared in Ashe's hands. The Indian screamed as he was lifted off his feet, a bloody hole appearing in his chest accompanied by a red mist. He was thrown backwards, spraying blood, and disappeared from sight. Ashe heard him fall on the other side of the rock. He darted forward and took up a position behind another rock, looking back the way he had come, searching for movement that would indicate the whereabouts of the second Indian, but he saw nothing.

The others, hearing the shot, were returning, calling his name and that's what he didn't want.

'Stay back. Make for the canyon,' he shouted.

'Ashe. What's going on?' It was the professor's voice.

'I'm all right. Keep going. I'll join you.' Ashe wasted no more breath. Shouting back and forth was only giving his position away. He squeezed between the rocks, hoping the professor would heed his words. Both Indians had been sent out to kill and it didn't matter which group it was.

Ashe clambered up until he was atop the rock cluster, then moved, keeping low, in the direction of the canyon. Leaping from rock to rock, his eyes ranged in all directions, looking for sign.

'Ashe, where are you?' The professor's voice was close and Ashe's heart skipped a beat. He moved forward and peered down. Ten feet below him stood the professor. The man was on foot. Ashe was ready to call out a warning when the spear caught the professor high on the left shoulder from the rear. It shattered bone before driving deep into muscle and sinew, an inch of bloody point emerging just below the collar bone.

The force of the throw sent the professor to his hands and knees, spectacles jolting from his nose, a cry of fear and pain bubbling from his lips. The Indian appeared seconds later, materializing from rocks ahead and across from where Ashe crouched. He came fast, knife in hand. He had not seen Ashe, his attention concentrated on the wounded man.

Ashe rose to his feet. The diminishing gap between the Indian and the professor made it impossible to use the shotgun. Instead he drew his Colt Lightning in a blur of speed and shouted. Almost on the professor, the Indian looked up. A dark figure outlined against the blue sky was the last thing the Indian saw. A bullet drilled a neat, red hole between his startled eyes and blew a stream of brain, blood and bone out through a fist-sized hole at the back. The Indian was slammed on to his back. Nerve spasms jerked at his limbs then he lay still.

Ashe reached the wounded man's side seconds later and helped him sit back on his haunches. The spear protruded obscenely from his back, heavily staining the left side of his grey coat, front and back, with blood.

'Professor.' Ashe looked into the white, pain-creased face and a wry smile tugged at the professor's trembling lips.

'I heard you shout, Ashe. My own stupid fault. Too used to giving orders than receiving them. My glasses, old boy, could you get them? Can't see a thing without them.'

Constance arrived with the others in tow; she paled at the sight of her father, the spear sticking from his back, then flew to his side and took over Ashe's position.

'Oh, Dad, Dad,' she crooned, tears filling her eyes.

'Don't fuss, Constance.' The professor managed to get a snap to his voice. Ashe retrieved the professor's spectacles, buffed them on his sleeve and slipped them on to the man's grey, sweating face. 'It'll have to come out?' he croaked, eyeing Ashe and Ashe nodded. He felt Constance's eyes on himself, but did not look at her. He turned to the Boyde brothers.

'Grey Dog only had two bucks with him, but there

mebbe more. I don't trust that old heathen. Get up on the rocks and keep a lookout. If there are more about they'll know the area, so keep low. Don't give 'em a target to go for.'

'Yes, sir,' they both chorused, glad to have something to do.

The professor had sunk into an uncomfortable sitting position against the kneeling Constance. His eyes had a glassy, dazed look and he was close to passing out, his breathing harsh and laboured.

Silas Boyde drew Ashe aside.

'What do we do, Ashe?' There was anxiety in his whispered words.

'Like the man says, it's gotta come out,' Ashe said and Silas grabbed his arm.

'Do you mean we do it?' He sounded more worried.

'Can't see no regular doctor, 'bout, can you?' Ashe said lightly. 'Help Constance keep him upright while I take a look.'

As carefully as he could Ashe used his knife to cut away the material of the man's coat and shirt from around the buried spear head. Even so, groans of pain fell from the man's shaking lips. Constance gasped as the area was exposed and Silas looked away. The weight of the shaft was causing every tiny movement to be magnified through the head of the spear. Ashe wiped his sweating brow with the back of his hand and rose to his feet. A few quick steps took him to where the Morgan patiently waited. Ashe ran a hand over the beast's velvet muzzle and whispered a few soothing words into its ear before removing the lariat from the saddlehorn and digging out a half bottle of whiskey from the saddle-bags. The whiskey he had picked up at the outlaws' camp.

Questions were in the eyes of Constance and Silas when he returned a few minutes later with the objects, but he said nothing. He tossed the rope aside and hunkered down before the professor, whiskey bottle in his hand. The man still had a stubborn grip on consciousness. For what was going to happen next it would have been better had he not.

'This is gonna hurt a mite, Professor,' he warned. 'Might help to take a pull on this.' He held the bottle out, but the man shook his head.

'Never touch the stuff. Get on with it, Ashe. Get the infernal thing out. It can't hurt more than it does.'

Ashe nodded and lifted his gaze to Constance and Silas.

'Take a good strong hold, folks.' He arose, knees popping, and moved behind the professor. His mouth was dry, hands shaking a little. Constance looked up at him with a tear-stained face, mutely begging him not to hurt her father. Ashe tried to comfort her with a reassuring smile that he did not feel. The smile faded as he took a two-handed grip on the spear shaft. He licked his lips and nodded at the two and then with one swift, sharp yank, pulled the spear from the man's shoulder.

It came out cleanly. The spear had been a flat sided hunting spear rather than a barbed war-spear that would have pulled the man's whole shoulder off.

The professor cried out as agony ripped with fingers of fire at his shoulder and then he slumped silently against Constance.

Blood erupted from the hole. Ashe tossed the spear aside and swiftly went to work. He poured whiskey into the wound and had the professor not been unconscious, he would have been after that fiery brew hit it. Next he pulled off his bandanna, folded it into a pad and instructed Silas to do the same with his. He placed the pad over the hole at the back and had Silas do the same at the front, then with Silas holding them both in place used the lariat. He turned it half a dozen times around the man's upper body to immobilize his left arm and hold the pads in place. It was all over in five minutes. As Ashe scoured blood from his hands with sand, Constance, clutching her unconscious father, looked at him.

'Will he be all right, Ashe?' Her voice shook.

'I've done all I can, ma'am. Figure he's a lot tougher than he looks. Reckon he's gotta good chance.'

She smiled her thanks and held her father close.

'He's in no state to be moved, Ashe,' Silas said softly as he crossed to Ashe's side.

'Mebbe not, but one thing's for sure, we can't stay here. We'll head into the canyon and find a place to hole up for a couple of days. Give his shoulder a chance to heal afore we move on.'

'You didn't trust Grey Dog from the start did you?'

'I still don't. That's why we need to find a safe place that we can defend, if needs be.'

'You think Grey Dog may have more braves?'

'Until I know different. Any sign of movement, boys?' He called up to Frank and Michael and got negative shakes of the head from both. 'Well come down now, we're moving out.' He turned to Silas. 'Gotta find a place afore the professor wakes up.'

They were an hour into the canyon, Ashe supporting the still unconscious professor before him on the Morgan, when they found the cave. Sheer red walls rose hundreds of feet into the air on either side of them, less than half a mile separating the walls. The cave, set into the west wall, had an entrance tall enough for a man to enter without ducking his head. Inside it went back twenty feet or so and looked to be the same wide. The floor was hard rock below a thin layer of red sand, but it was the surprise extra feature that made it perfect. A thin trickle of water ran from a crack in the rear wall into a shallow, circular basin some two feet across. The overflow from the basin disappeared underground. Ashe tasted the water. It was cool and fresh with the taste of nectar.

'Best hotel in town, I'd say, Ashe,' Silas Boyde joked as they made the professor comfortable on the hard floor of the cave. Ashe changed the blood soaked bandannas for fresh dressings, using strips of Constance's petticoat that she had kept, for pads and bandages. That done they wrapped him in blankets, the rest was up to the professor himself. It was soon after that that the Boyde brothers burst excitedly into the cave, for they had remained outside to take a look around.

'You just gotta see this, Dad, Ashe,' Michael gasped. 'It's incredible.'

'You too, Constance,' Frank moved to her side.

'I can't leave Dad,' she protested.

'He'll be out for a while yet,' Ashe pointed out.

'And it's not far, just up the canyon a-ways. Fact is you can see this cave from where we're going.' Frank was anxious to show her.

Constance smiled wanly.

'I guess it won't harm none,' she relented and found herself between the two brothers, being propelled from the cave.

Outside the cave the canyon floor climbed gently as it continued north. Ashe and Silas followed Constance and the two boys until a hundred yards from the cave they crested the rise and came to a halt. The eyes of the three popped at the sight that lay before them. Michael's words had not done it justice.

Before them, as the ground sloped away, the canyon walls on either side opened out and the snaking, half-mile width they had followed to the cave became five or six miles. It was no longer a canyon but a huge, walled valley that spread ahead of them for as far as the eye could see and filled with rock formations the like of which Ashe had never seen before.

At the base of the cliff walls on either side, huge spires of red rose from the blood-hued sand. Thick at the base, they rose to delicate, tapering points a hundred feet above the ground. As these rocks spires moved outwards they grew smaller. Mingling with them huge buttresses of rock thrust from the cliff face showing the effects of ancient, raging winds that must have once blasted the canyon. All were weathered and smooth, some carved by the scouring winds into high, soaring archways.

Further towards the centre of the incredible valley a twisting spine of broken rock crawled like some huge, half-buried worm into the distance, its shattered outcrops sculpted by the wind into strange shapes bored through with holes. It was about this central rock formation, that appeared and disappeared as it crawled brokenly into the distance, that lay the biggest surprise.

'My God!' The words fell from Silas Boyde's lips as his popping eyes took in the incredible sight. Across the centre of the valley and stretching away into the distance rose line after line of high, wooden platforms, each supported on spindly, wooden legs.

They had found the burial ground.

Only Ashe remained outwardly unmoved by the spectacle, but inwardly his stomach knotted as ten-year-old memories flooded back.

NINE

His name was Cal Baker. Together with Ashe, the pair roamed the Nevadan plains and valleys, dodging Indians as they looked for gold. Friends from way back, the desolation and hostility of the land forged an even stronger friendship as they came to depend on each other to stay alive. Of a similar build, Cal was blond to Ashe's dark and where Ashe was cautious, Cal was the exact opposite: always smiling and happy-go-lucky. In towns they would drink and womanize and listen to the old-timers tell their stories and that was when they first heard of the Burial Ground.

'There's gold there fer sure,' the old-timer said, nodding, a faraway look in his button-black eyes. 'Trouble is there's Injuns too.'

'Injuns don't worry me an' my pard here,' Cal bragged, and a thin smile tugged at the old-timer's lips.

'Ain't the live ones you gotta look out fer, son, it's the dead ones.'

Outside the saloon a buffeting night wind rattled loose boards and creaked the batwings open.

Cal and Ashe exchanged amused glances.

'Reckon you bin on the gut-rot too long, old fella,' Cal said with a laugh. 'Never knowed a dead Injun to be any trouble at all.'

'That's 'cause you don't know the old Shoshoni burial ground.' The old-timer shivered and downed his whiskey in a single gulp. There was no laughter in his eyes, only bad memories.

'Figure it's a place to know if'n there's gold there,' Cal said, and this time the old-timer smiled, but the smile never reached his eyes.

'Forget it, son. That place ain't nothin' but grief.'

Ashe eyed his friend and knew that he was not going to forget it ...

'Ashe, Ashe.' A tugging at his sleeve chased the vivid memories away. He shook his head and stared into the concerned eyes of Constance. 'Where were you, Ashe?' she asked.

'I can understand how he feels,' Silas Boyde broke in. 'Magnificent isn't it?' He mistook Ashe's memory trip for awe. 'Let's get back to the cave: George may be awake and wondering where everyone is. Wait till he hears about this.'

'Well tell me about it.' The professor, pale faced sat propped against the outer wall of the cave. Outside, night had long since fallen, filling the canyon with smothering darkness. Earlier a small cook fire had been lit outside the cave to provide the group with hot food and coffee, but this was now out, Ashe not wishing to draw unnecessary attention to the cave.

A lambent, golden glow filled the cave, thinning to a shadow hung gloom as it stretched to the rear wall. The glow came from an oil lamp that Ashe had brought along on the pack-mule. Through long experience he had deemed the item a necessity on long, lonely trips into the desolate, Nevadan backwaters. He had slept rough in caves before and knew the comfort a lamp could bring. That and a small container of oil always made up the basic items on the pack-mule.

'It was only a preliminary look, George,' Silas Boyde said regretfully. He sat cross-legged opposite the professor with Frank and Michael flanking him. Constance was away from the group, sorting through the contents of the bags on the pack-mule. 'Tomorrow we'll take a closer look.' He looked up at Ashe who was standing to one side of the group. 'That'll be no problem will it, Ashe? You said yourself we'll be here a coupla days while George's wound heals. Might as well make use of the time.'

'Don't see no reason agin it,' Ashe replied. 'Just as long as you keep your eyes peeled. Strikes me that that old medicine man may have a trick or two up his sleeve for us yet. For that reason I suggest we set up a rota of night watches while we're here.'

'Point taken, Ashe,' Silas agreed.

'Confound this shoulder, stopping me from going with you,' the professor moaned.

'On the contrary, George. It's that shoulder that is giving us the opportunity to take a look at the burial ground,' Silas pointed out.

'I'd rather not have been the silver lining to this particular cloud,' the professor said grumpily. 'But tell me more of what you saw.'

Ashe drifted out of the cave with a rifle while the three repeated their first impressions of the burial ground. To the right of the cave entrance a cluster of rocks formed an ideal position to watch from. He settled in the rocks and his mind drifted.

The old-timer had said a lot that night. Strange, unbelievable tales of a shadowy, unreal world where the dead ruled the living and the ghosts walked the night. Others in the saloon had heard the stories before and a lot of ridicule was heaped on the old-timer's head, but the old man refused to be put off by it. He knew what he knew and no one was going to tell him any different. Cal laughed with the others, but there was gold fever in his eyes and Ashe had to admit to himself that he felt the same. It was a pity they hadn't heeded the old-timer's words and maybe Cal would have been alive today ...

'You've gone again, Ashe.'

The voice startled Ashe. He snapped his head around and found Constance standing a few feet from him. He had not seen or heard her emerge from the cave.

'Ma'am,' he acknowledged her presence glad of the darkness that hid the taut lines setting his features hard and grim.

'You've been here before haven't you, Ashe?'

'Wouldn't have knowed where to bring you if'n I hadn't,' he replied lightly, refusing to be drawn.

'I mean here; this cave. I get the impression you knew it was here before we entered the canyon, but you didn't say.'

'Ma'am, I didn't want to come here in the first place, but I guess a man don't always have control over his fate. I won't be happy until we're all out of here.'

Just detectable in his voice was an emotion that Constance found hard to believe in the big man; fear. Not naked, cringing fear, but controlled, imprisoned fear that she could not understand. She had seen him face Indians and outlaws at less than even odds to himself without turning a hair, yet he was afraid and that fear could only be of this place itself. Was he afraid of ghosts and demons? The idea was laughable. Something had happened the last time he had been here that now made him more than a little uneasy to have returned. She did not pursue the subject, but it came to her that if he was scared then maybe she should be too.

'Do you think we'll have any trouble tonight?'

'Never can tell with Indians, but I aim to be ready for it if we do.'

They talked for a while longer then Constance returned to the cave, troubled, but not showing it. Ashe had revealed a side of himself that was as enigmatic as this place.

* * *

It had never been really clear what had happened to Cal. The second day there he had disappeared.

They had found a vein of gold in a shallow cave. Leaving Cal there Ashe had returned to where they had camped, this very cave where the group now sheltered. He had returned for a second pick and on arriving back, Cal had gone. Ashe had spent the rest of the day searching for his friend, but had found no trace. The old-timer had spoken of men who had gone there with the glint of gold in their eyes never to return, but Ashe had put their non-return down to them being killed by the Indians. Of the many tales the old-timer had to tell had been one when a man was found wandering, his mind gone, in the desert. All he spoke of was the ghosts of the dead that he had seen.

He had laughed at the absurdity of it at the time, whiskey making the old-timer's tales more fantastic as the night wore on. He didn't laugh now, not after what he had seen that day.

Ashe spent the night restlessly in the cave, unable to sleep, hoping that at any moment Cal would appear with that familiar laugh and innocent, wide-eyed look. What sleep he managed to get was light catnaps between long periods of wakefulness.

At dawn he returned to the burial ground only to find that it was filled with a cold, grey fog. His normally good-natured horse, a big red then, seemed nervous as it entered the mist, flicking its head and snorting. Ashe could feel the animal's reluctance, but kneed it forward all the same.

As they passed between and beneath the platforms of the dead the red's reluctance increased, the snorts turning to short, troubled whinnies. He had never seen the horse so jittery before. Something that it sensed rather than saw was spooking it. He brought the horse to a halt, patting its neck as he pulled the Winchester from its boot. Something hidden in the fog ahead. Puma maybe or wolf. Perhaps even man; redman!

Ashe slid from the saddle and stood still, listening. At first he heard nothing then he caught the sound of slow hooves thudding accompanied by the faint jingle of harness. He levered a shell into the breech and waited tensely. It could be Indians, but Indians don't ride with jingling harness. He heard the ring of a shod hoof on stone and knew that Indians didn't ride shod horses either.

Mouth dry he stood his ground realizing it could be a trick. Cal's horse had vanished. Maybe they were bringing it back, trying to lull him into a false sense of security. At any second a dozen Indians could burst upon him from the thick fog. His heart quickened. There was movement in the mist ahead.

He recognized the white blaze on the bay's head as it materialized from the fog as Cal's horse.

'Cal!' The name exploded from Ashe's lips in a wave of relief. 'Where the hell have you been? Man I oughta kick your damn ass ...' His voice faded. The slumped figure in the saddle, hatted head tipped forward, gave no response to Ashe's cry and

Ashe felt his nerves tighten again. He caught the bridle of the bay and brought it to a halt. Cal's hands were gripping the saddlehorn. 'Cal, are you hurt?' Ashe moved forward and gripped Cal's arm, shaking it gently. 'Cal?' The still, slumped figure slowly toppled towards him.

Ashe dropped his rifle and caught the falling figure. The hat fell from its head revealing a mass of blond hair that Ashe recognized as belonging to Cal. He gently lowered the figure to the ground laying it on its back.

'Jesus, Cal …' Ashe began, then he sprang up, heart pumping wildly, words choking in his throat, sweat breaking out over his face.

The face that stared sightlessly up bore only the vaguest resemblance to the ever-smiling, carefree Cal he knew. Fear had twisted the features into a grotesque, staring mask. The laughing mouth that had sweet-talked many a hesitant lady into his bed was now a gaping slit, lips pulled back in a feral snarl as though he had been screaming at the moment of death. Whatever he had seen now lay imprisoned in those dead staring eyes forever.

Ashe ran a trembling hand across his face. A faint sound snapped his head up and his own eyes opened in the same terror that filled the dead man's. Ahead of him, cloaked in the fog stood something that had once been human. Rotted clothes barely covered its fleshless ribs. Strips of dried flesh hung about a grinning skull face. Ragged, empty eye sockets seemed to stare ghoulishly at him. As he stared at the impossible thing a second wobbled into view, a patch of dark hair clinging stubbornly to the skull hanging down over its bone face.

Frozen with a fear he had never known Ashe stood rooted to the spot until a tiny spark of sanity broke through the terrible paralysis. With a gurgling cry Ashe drew his Colt Lightning and triggered shot after shot at the hellish abominations. Skull and bone exploded, shattering as the bullets found their mark.

Ashe's memory of events after that were of a vague, mindless flight through the fog-shrouded burial ground, fleeing in terror from a nightmare that had claimed his friend's life. Now he was back and so were the terrible memories as vivid and real as though they had just happened ...

Ashe was glad when the dawn finally came and the daylight chased the night horrors away. The professor was feeling much better and the wound was healing nicely. Ashe redressed it while Constance and the Boyde brothers lit a fire and prepared breakfast. After an uneventful night and fully rested the group were in high spirits.

'I can ride there and just sit,' the professor said as later, breakfast over, plans were being made to go to the burial ground.

'The wound's healing nicely, Professor, but you ride any distance on a horse an' it'll open up agin,' Ashe said and the professor pulled a face.

'But I can't just sit here doing nothing, blast it,'

he exploded.

'Ashe is right, Father and you know it,' Constance broke in. 'I'll stay with you and you won't be on your own.'

'And if we find any small objects of interest I'll make sure they are brought to you for study and evaluation,' Silas Boyde promised and the professor brightened at that.

'That's a wonderful idea,' the professor enthused, nodding. 'At least I'll be making some contribution.' He glanced slyly at Ashe. 'Of course, if we were to stay a week or two …'

'We move out the day after tomorrow,' Ashe replied obstinately. 'For one thing I don't think Grey Dog is going to sit by an' let us stay here without trying something. He's a murderous old Indian an' like as not he's gotta few more around him of a like mind. Secondly, we ain't got enough food for a prolonged stay.'

'Damnation, Ashe,' the professor moaned.

'That's 'bout where we'll end up if we stay,' Ashe said grimly.

'What are you gonna do while we're at the burial ground, Ashe?' Silas Boyde asked.

'Take a look around. If'n there's Indians around I'll find their sign. Just you folks keep a good lookout. The Indians take their sacred ground seriously, judging by the two braves Grey Dog put on our tail. They won't be afraid to die for it an' be mighty proud to kill for it.'

'We'll look out for ourselves,' Silas promised.

Ashe turned his gaze on Constance.

'The same applies here, ma'am. Keep a gun close by at all times while I'm gone.'

'You worry too much, Ashe,' she chided with a smile, but his face remained deadly serious.

'Worried folks tend to stay alive longer,' he replied. 'I'll be seeing you folks later.' He tipped his hat to Constance and left the cave, carrying his saddle out to the Morgan.

The sun was pouring over the eastern rim of the canyon as Ashe rode back the way they had come. He followed the tracks they had made on the way in, his eyes were searching for others. If they had been followed into the canyon he wanted to know by how many.

He had ridden perhaps a mile when the single shot rang out. It came from the direction he had just ridden from. He turned the Morgan and dug his heels into its ribs. The animal responded magnificently. Head stretched forward it galloped back towards the cave.

Constance was standing in the entrance rifle in hand when Ashe drew the Morgan to a slithering halt.

'What's going on?'

'It wasn't me, Ashe. The shot came from the burial ground.'

A shiver ran through him.

'I'll take a look. Stay here and keep your eyes open.' Ashe didn't wait for an answer. He urged the Morgan forward, a cold feeling of dread gripping him.

He crested the rise in the trail and an incredible

sight met his eyes. A thick white fog filled the walled valley of the burial ground. It hid the slender legs supporting the platforms of the dead until it seemed as though the platforms floated on top of the still, unmoving fog. It was an eerie, unnerving sight. Overhead the sky was a deep blue. He could feel the hot sun beating against his right side as he sat there astride the Morgan. It reflected whitely from the fog bank. Soon it would burn the fog away, until then it would be a different world for those wrapped in the cold, clammy fog.

Another shot, closer this time, made the Morgan quiver between his legs. It sounded like a hand gun. Ashe quietened the animal and gripped the Winchester tighter, feeling the dryness of fear in his throat. Ten years had not quelled the horror of that day.

The edge of the fog bank lay some fifty feet from where he waited. He heard scuffling sounds. A shape appeared, grey and indistinct. The Morgan whickered and moved uneasily.

Michael Boyde burst from the fog and went sprawling in the sand, the Colt spinning from his hand. The boy had not seen Ashe. Small, terrified whimpers fell from his lips, reaching Ashe's ears.

Ashe slid from the saddle.

'Michael!' He shouted the name as he plunged down the slope towards the youngster.

Something moved on the edge of the fog bank. Ashe caught a glimpse of something man-shaped and almost the same colour as the fog. Dark ragged eye sockets did register as he aimed the Winchester, fired, reloaded and fired again. Whatever it was disappeared back into the fog by the time the second bullet was on its way. The fog was shrinking fast as Ashe slid a hand beneath the youngster's arm and hauled him up on to rubbery legs.

'Where are the others? Silas, Frank?' Ashe's heart contracted. The eyes of Michael Boyde were wide and staring. If the boy hadn't reached madness yet he was only one step away. 'Michael, can you hear me? It's Ashe.' He gentled his voice.

'Ashe?' Michael loked confused. He gripped Ashe's arms with weak, trembling hands.

'What's happened to Silas and Frank?'

The fear that was fading from Michael's eyes flooded back. He stared towards the thinning fog, lips trembling.

'They came, Ashe.' His voice was a broken whisper.

'Who came, Michael?'

Michael Boyde looked at Ashe.

'The dead. They came and took them away!'

TEN

'What's the matter with him, Ashe?' Constance asked in a shocked whisper, looking across to where Michael Boyde sat huddled in a corner wrapped in a blanket, his body wracked with shudders. He had remained there, unspeaking, since Ashe had brought him back to the cave.

'He's in deep shock.' The professor had hauled himself to his feet. Arm in a sling and on shaky legs he moved towards the pair.

'Father, you shouldn't be up,' she remonstrated.

'Hush, girl, don't fuss,' the professor barked. 'If I lay on my back much longer you'll have to carry me out of here. What happened to him, Ashe?'

'Only he can tell you that, Professor,' Ashe replied bleakly. He ran a hand across his bristly chin. He thought he could handle the horrors of Spirit Canyon. He had done so ever since being forced by circumstances to come to this lonely, God-forsaken place. He could handle the memories and the nightmares. It was when nightmare became reality that he felt himself slipping.

'What about Silas and Frank?' the professor asked.

It was on the tip of Ashe's tongue to say forget them and let's get out of here while we can, but he fought the urge.

'I don't know,' he replied tightly.

'But you'll look for them?'

Ashe's eyes met those of the professor's. In them he read a total belief and faith in his, Ashe's ability to make everything come right. His gaze flickered to Constance. She had the same belief. They were totally dependant on him and all he wanted to do was run. He took a tight rein on his emotions.

'Sure, I'll take a look, but if I can't find 'em then we get out of here as fast as we can,' he replied dully, hating the fear that was eating into him, destroying him, turning him into someone to be ashamed of.

'But you must find them,' the professor insisted.

Anger was beginning to well up inside when a figure darkened the cave entrance. Constance gave a shriek and Ashe spun, levelling the rifle as Grey Dog, the medicine man, entered the cave. There was no fear in the old, wrinkled face. He walked across to where Michael sat, stared at the boy for a few seconds before turning, crossing his arms imperiously across his chest and staring coldly at Ashe.

'The demons have his soul. Too late for him. You leave now,' he commanded.

'You got gall, old man, I'll say that for you,' Ashe complimented tautly. 'How many braves you bring with you this time?'

'Grey Dog travel alone. Spirits protect him.'

Ashe's eyes narrowed.

'Reckon we'll have to check on that. Move out, old man.' He gestured with the rifle. Grey Dog eyed him contemptuously then unfolded his arms and moved out of the cave. Ashe followed cautiously, eyes twitching left and right as he paused in the cave entrance. The only sign of life in the canyon was the scraggy pinto the old man had rode in on. Ashe's eyes raked the ground for sign, but the old man had come alone.

'The boy has looked into the eyes of the dead. Soon he will die,' Grey Dog said facing Ashe again, arms once more folded across his chest. 'The spirits are angry.'

'I'm a mite pissed off myself,' Ashe replied tightly. 'Why are you here, old man?'

'To warn you that death is close. Unless you leave now you will die.'

'Well that's right neighbourly of you,' Ashe replied sarcastically. 'Now why don't you ride out of here before you join your ancestors.'

A sly smile tugged at the old man's leathery lips.

'Two of your number have already joined the spirit world. Soon you will join them.' He said no more as without a glance he headed back the way he had come. Ashe, with Constance at his side, watched him ride away.

'How did he know that Silas and Frank were missing, Ashe?'

'Because they weren't here. That old man's up to something. Let's get back in the cave.'

'What do you make of it, Ashe?' the professor

asked after the two had joined him.

'Figure he was just getting us primed up, playing on our nerves with all that crazy talk about spirits and demons.' Ashe was suddenly feeling better. If Grey Dog needed to come in and work on their nerves then maybe it was less spirit and more human agency at work here. 'The old man's trying to spook us.'

'Well he's doing a good job,' Constance replied.

'I'm going out to the burial ground, take a good look around. Keep on your guard, ma'am. I'll be as quick as I can.'

'You will be careful, Ashe?' Constance said anxiously.

'Depend on it,' he said confidently.

If Grey Dog's visit had promoted a fresh rush of rationalism, what Ashe found ten minutes later caused a positive surge.

Blood!

It splattered the ground in the vicinity where Ashe had fired at the half seen figure in the fog. Hasty attempts had been made to erase it, but there was still enough for him to recognize.

A grim smile broke across his face. To his way of thinking ghosts didn't bleed. Whatever he was up against it was taking on more human form.

He followed a trail of blood spots, brown stains on the stony sand, and weaving, indistinct footprints. Twenty yards further on a heat shimmering rock slab showed a sizeable stain, the

Burial Ground

ground about churned by many feet. Ashe read the signs on the ground and a picture evolved. The figure in the fog had been hit and badly too judging by the amount of blood. He had managed to stagger this far, fallen and then others had arrived on the scene and carried him away. Ashe stared around with his tawny eyes.

He was on the southern edge of the vast burial ground, the nearest of the tall, creaking platforms less than ten yards away. The ground became soft, red sand ahead with no mark of hurried, passing feet. To his left and right ran a reef of stone and sand, stony enough to hide footprints. He cast around, studying the ground and his sharp eyes noted the droplets of dried blood scattered about. Leading the Morgan Ashe followed the droplets towards the western wall.

Soon he was engulfed in a maze of low, rocky hills and ravines that split the ravaged ground between the thick based, stone columns. He followed a faint trail that twisted around the soaring stone spires and flowed beneath graceful, stone arches, all a deep, Hadean red.

Fans of red dust sprayed from the rock ledges as the light wind suddenly sprang up from nowhere. It had been blowing in fitful gusts for several minutes before Ashe realized it, so intent had he been on studying the ground that showed unshod hoof prints. He raised his head in frustration as the puffs and pants of the wind erased the tracks.

As the gusty wind strengthened the air became filled with gritty dust that put a halo of red about the sun and turned the blue sky a muddy brown. He pulled a yellow bandanna, that had replaced the one used as a pad on the professor's wound, to cover his nose and lower face, cursing the wind. The rocks and spires around him appeared and disappeared behind clouds of flying dust. The wind grew stronger, pummelling his hunched back and hissing in his ears. It stung where it touched flesh, the sand giving it an abrasive quality. Then above the hiss he heard it and his blood ran cold.

A triple moaning sound filled his ears, rising and falling. A ghostly wailing sound that seemed to be all around him. The Morgan tensed beneath him, for now he rode the animal, and it snorted its alarm, ears twitching. Ashe remembered Grey Dog's words about the rocks singing and the supernatural terrors struggled to regain their hold of him. Then he realized that the sound was nothing more than the wind in the high ramparts and tall, rock spires and his fears evaporated. He patted the Morgan's sleek neck, spoke softly and felt the animal relax beneath him. It was not unusual for winds, fueled by the heat, to spring up suddenly in country such as this.

Constance and the professor listened to the wind from the sheltered safety of the cave. Constance moved back from the entrance, where she had paced restlessly since Ashe's departure, as billows of reddish, gritty dust darted in. The professor, shoulder beset with a dull ache, wandered across to Michael Boyde. The youngster had not moved since Ashe had brought him in. He just sat there, hugging his knees and staring at nothing. Even the entrance of Grey Dog had not touched him. The professor spent a few moments trying to talk his way through the shell the youngster had built around himself, but gave up as he got no response.

'The shock is too deep,' he murmured to Constance, shaking his head mournfully. 'Whatever he saw has closed his mind off to reality.' He eased himself down on to a flat rock, wincing at his throbbing shoulder. He didn't like to dwell on what horrors the young man had seen, but he feared the worst for Silas and Frank.

'You should rest, Dad,' Constance reproached him.

'I'm all right, girl. Don't fuss. I've rested enough,' he protested tartly.

Constance moved back further from the entrance rubbing grit from her eyes.

'The wind's getting stronger. Can't see a thing out there with all that dust. I hope Ashe is all right.' She snapped her head up as a low, multiple wail reached her ears and bored in waves of coldness into her soul. Like Ashe, the chilling words of Grey Dog sprang to mind. Her eyes flickered nervously about the gloomy cave, heart racing.

The professor cocked an ear.

'It's the wind,' he said, noting his daughter's look. 'Just the sound of the wind, nothing more.'

'Well, I wish Ashe were back,' she said

dry-mouthed. Her palms were clammy holding the shotgun. The weapon felt heavy in her grip. She peered at the swirling, eddying dust clouds that blew across the cave entrance like a ragged, dirty curtain; sometimes in thick, dark billows, other times, wispy, ragged streamers.

She gave a hoarse gasp, throat constricting, ice settling in her stomach. Something had moved momentarily into view just beyond the entrance, then the dust had enveloped it.

'Ashe! Is that you?' she gasped, peering intently, then her eye bulged and she screamed, the sound of terror echoing from wall to wall.

'Constance!' The professor came to his feet, unnerved by her scream as things emerged from the dust and entered the cave. She saw white, bloodless bodies and dark, gaping eye sockets. Dead things that had once been human now imbued with hellish life. The shotgun fell from her nerveless fingers. The nightmarish scene before her wavered and went black as she dropped to the floor in a faint.

Her scream had reached into Michael's locked mind, his head turned and animation returned to his vacant face. Whimpers of terror fell from his shaking lips.

The professor stared with popping eyes at the terrible apparitions as they advanced silently towards him. He sank to his knees thrusting a hand as if to ward them off.

'No,' he croaked. 'No!'

Burial Ground

* * *

Ashe rested out of the wind and let tears wash the stinging grit from his eyes before brushing them from his cheeks.

After riding blind for almost twenty minutes he had come upon an area where the high, red cliffs folded like the pleats in some huge curtain. He had ridden into one such pleat and found himself on a narrow, twisting path that wormed deep into the rock. The sheer walls that towered far above him to a tiny thread of blue gripped him in a claustrophobic squeeze.

The walls crowded in and wrapped him in a shroud of gloom. He continued doggedly on until the narrowing walls forced him to dismount and lead the Morgan. He had exchanged the abrasive, howling dust for a funereal silence haunted only by the low, melancholy lament of a wind he could not feel. The Morgan's metal shod hooves rang and echoed as they struck stone.

Ashe was beginning to feel that he had made a mistake in penetrating so far when the way ahead grew lighter. He pushed on and a few minutes later emerged into a circular opening that proved to be the base of a wide rock chimney that rose up through the heart of the cliff.

The area before him was perhaps a quarter of a mile across, but seemed smaller in the soaring enclosure of rock. Clumps of tired looking brush carpeted the sandy floor. The base of the chimney presented an amazing spectacle to his reddened eyes. Erosion had gouged a deep channel in the rock that led back into dark, shadow-hung depths. In places the erosion had not been complete. Squat, stone pillars had been left rising from ground to overhang to give the whole a cloister-like appearance.

In the warm, still air, the smell of horse droppings was the last aroma Ashe thought to sniff, but it was strong in his flaring nostrils. The Morgan whickered and an answering snort from the right pricked up the animal's ears. One area below the erosion-formed overhang had been roped off to form a crude corral and half a dozen mustangs stood shoulder to shoulder peering out at the new arrival in the shape of the Morgan.

A surge of excitement coursed through Ashe. Spirit Canyon was becoming less ghostly the more he saw of it. He left the Morgan knowing that the animal would stay there and crossed to the corral. Unshod Indian mustangs. Ashe peered warily around, drawing his Colt Lightning. The way in also seemed to be the way out. He could find himself trapped. He wondered where the owners of the mustangs were.

Something came at him from the darkness at the rear of the overhang. He caught a vague blur of white out of the corner of one eye and turned and his heart lurched. The white shape with huge, black eye sockets looked like something out of a nightmare. For one heart-stopping moment Ashe thought he was facing a living corpse. Dark eyes sparkled hatefully in the centres of the black eye sockets. The thing was nothing more than a man painted white from head to foot with eyes and mouth outlined in black.

The figure clutched a tomahawk as it closed on Ashe. Ashe saw white painted lips open in the white face and the yipping cry of triumph became a death cry as the Colt Lightning exploded in Ashe's hand.

Impetus carried the man forward, blood spraying from his lips and splashing down his white chest. Ashe leapt aside as the Indian crashed past him, jerking convulsively as he hit the ground.

With screams and yells more figures appeared. A spear flew past his head making his next shot miss. He didn't get another chance. A body crashed against him and he went sprawling back out on to the sand, the Colt Lightning spinning from his hand. Ashe managed to regain his feet to face four protagonists closing in on him. He was drawing his knife, ready to make a stand, when he became aware of a fifth, but by then it was too late. Something slammed hard against the back of his head and his world went black.

Ashe returned to consciousness through a welter of throbbing pain. He lifted his head from his chest and found himself in a cave lit by a series of burning torches set in cracks around the walls. He was sitting against a wall and it took him some seconds to realize that his arms were stretched out on either side, wrists bound to wooden stakes anchored in fissures in the wall. He shook his head. His back and buttocks were stiff from sitting in the same position for a long time. He had no way of knowing how long.

A hand took a handful of his hair and slammed the back of his head against the rock sending shards of pain lancing into his brain. He found himself looking into a grinning, white face. His hair was released. the figure vanished and a few minutes later returned in the company of Grey Dog and other white-painted braves.

Grey Dog planted himself before Ashe, arms folded across his skinny chest. Moving shadows from the flickering torches played on his lined features.

'Spirit Canyon sacred to Shoshoni. My white warriors guard the dead. White man and his friends must die for entering sacred place. Make spirits happy, make demons happy.'

'Where are the others?' Ashe asked dully.

'We have all strangers in the House of Bones. Soon they die, but for you special death.' He smiled and the accompanying white faces smiled. 'Bring him!'

Ashe was cut free but it was a short-lived freedom for his wrists were bound again before him. Torches were gathered and he was led from the cave down a short tunnel and into a smaller cave. In the guttering light he was led towards a pit some ten feet across in the centre of the floor. A number of the torches were tossed into the pit and what he saw at the bottom froze his blood.

Thirty feet below him lit by the flickering, uncertain light of the torches that had been flung down, a bizarre nightmarish scene greeted his eyes. A series of man-high, wooden stakes, their tips whittled to needle-sharp points waited in silent anticipation, but that was not the immediate cause of the initial shock. Someone with a taste for the grotesque had been at work. Skeletons, probably previous victims of the pit, had been arranged so that they seemed to be holding the stakes. Heads tipped back, jaws gaping in a soundless laugh, their black, eyeless sockets stared up at the next victim.

'Spirit warriors wait for you,' Grey Dog intoned. 'Soon you will be one of them.'

Ashe stiffened in the hands holding him, heart pounding, waiting for the thrust that would send him hurtling down on to the waiting points. Instead he was pulled back from the edge and his ankles lashed. Next a rope was run across his chest, under the arms and knotted in a loop at his back. Finally he was led back to the pit. A long piece of timber had been heaved into position over the drop. Its base rested in a depression on the edge of the abyss while its top found anchorage in a niche in the roof. In position it lay at an angle over the pit. The rope was passed over a notch cut in the timber and a few seconds later Ashe found himself swinging above the pointed stakes, hands and feet bound. He was lowered down about ten feet before the rope was tied off leaving him dangling there.

He didn't have long to wait to find out what was going to happen next. A burning torch was lashed at right angles to the rope holding him and animal fat rubbed into the rope where the two met. He craned his head up. There was about three inches of the torch to burn before it reached the rope. With a sinking heart he realized he had maybe an hour left to live.

ELEVEN

Sweat inched from Ashe's hairline and ran a weaving, itching course down his face. The rope cut into his armpits and lay tight across his chest. He was alone. Grey Dog and his white warriors had departed some time ago to leave him to contemplate the final horror to come when the flames burnt through the rope to plunge him on to the stakes below. He peered down at the white, bone faces looking up at him. Soon the torches in the pit would burn out and darkness would blot out the awful scene below, but it would not be blotted out in his mind.

The torches in the pit flickered fitfully filling it with restless moving shadows that seemed to make the dead things below him move in a jerky, macabre dance. He stared around in desperation and his eyes became drawn to a spot where one stake appeared to be missing. If it could be reached there was just enough room for a man to drop into the gap left by the missing stake. The only problem was that he was suspended over the centre of pit and the gap that beckoned teasingly was on the edge.

He studied it. It was possible if he had the nerve to try something really crazy. One of the torches thrown into the pit went out and the flames were dimming on the others. It was either now or never. At least this way there was a chance. If he waited it was certain death.

Licking dry lips Ashe lifted his arms and made a grab for the rope behind his head. As he did so he began to slip through the loop. His bound hands gripped the rope and halted his slide. He shook sweat from his eyes as the pounding of his own heart filled his ears. He came to the conclusion that he was crazy, but it was too late for him to do anything about it now, he was committed.

He eased the grip and let himself slide gently down the rope until his hands reached the knot of the loop. He continued his slide until his hands were hooked over the bottom loop. Below him another torch spluttered out. Now only two remained. The shadows lengthened and darkness thickened in the bottom of the pit. He thrust the thoughts of what could happen to him if this went wrong from his mind, filling it with happy visions of himself throttling Grey Dog, and began to swing.

The rope creaked above him as he swung back and forth. Then there was a sudden increase in light. He looked up, the rope was flaring brightly. His pendulum swing had blown the flames on to the rope.

He swung back towards the gap and as the wall of the pit rushed towards him he released his grip on the burning rope and dropped.

He hit the wall of the pit with his body and a second later his forehead. With stars exploding before his eyes he felt himself sliding down the wall then falling backwards. His bound feet hit the ground as he fell.

Ancient, fragile bones shattered beneath his falling body before he was brought up short by slamming into a stake. The breath went from his body as he tipped sideways and fell heavily on to his right side, bringing a skeleton crashing down over him. He lay there for several minutes, pulling dusty air into his gasping lungs. Finally he hauled himself upright. He had made it.

The third torch went out leaving just one a few yards to his right. Bending he unfastened the rope at his ankles. To his left he had seen a small opening and he guessed that that was the way Grey Dog came and went from the pit after arranging the skeletons. He had already realized there was air flowing into the pit bottom by the way the torch flames flickered and was hoping that offered a way out.

He moved to the edge of the opening. The rock was rough and sharp. He worked his bound wrists back and forth until his arms were free, the effort causing him to breathe heavily.

The burning rope parted and fell into the centre of the pit. He moved back to where the final torch spluttered and hissed, grabbed it up and returned to the opening. The tunnel within, no more than three feet high, angled steeply upward. Ashe scrambled up and came out in the tunnel between the cave where he had first woken up and the pit cave. He was pondering on his next move when he heard movement from the first cave. Light flickered at that end of the tunnel. Ashe tossed his torch back down the tunnel connecting to the pit bottom and eased himself back into the darkness and waited.

The Indian, his body still covered in white, padded past the hidden Ashe heading towards the pit. Ashe followed silently. The Indian was peering down into the pit when Ashe came up behind him. At the last second the Indian became aware of his presence, but by then it was too late. Ashe grabbed the knife from the Indian's belt as the man turned. A flaming torch was thrust at Ashe's face. He ducked and rammed a fist into the white stomach.

The Indian screamed out in terror as he overbalanced and plunged down into the pit. The screams died to a death gurgle as the sharpened stakes punctured his body in three places and drove upwards and out through his chest and stomach. When Ashe looked the luckless man was slowly sliding down the blood drenched stakes that impaled his twitching body. Ashe felt no remorse. It was the fate that they had planned for him.

It was the monotonous beat of a lone drum that drew Ashe to the cavern. In truth he had become lost in a maze of tunnels until the drum started up. Even then it had taken him some time to reach the source of the lone drummer.

The cavern was huge. A good half a mile across and perhaps a hundred feet high. Stalactites hung

Burial Ground

from the domed roof and in places formed complete columns from floor to roof. Ashe thought that after all he had seen and endured, there was nothing left in Spirit Canyon to surprise or amaze him. He was wrong! The scene that greeted his eyes in the enormous cavern came direct from a nightmare.

A huge, cathedral-like beam of sunlight angled down from a hidden hole in the roof, striking an area that was roughly the centre of the cavern. It spread its golden light in all directions, thinning as it moved outwards and throwing shadows from the massive rocks that littered the floor. Where shadows and darkness merged, torches had been set around and it was in this flickering, uncertain light that the huge bones and monstrous rib cages that littered the cavern showed up.

Ashe had never seen anything to match their sizes before. Rib cages that a man could stand upright in. Fearsome, reptilian skulls, gaping mouths filled with razor sharp teeth snarled silently amid the dancing shadows. The single drummer sat cross-legged on a plinth of rock some eight feet high, drum nestling in the well of his legs. Other members of Grey Dog's White Warriors sat in the wide circle encompassing the drummer and a central dais. It was on the dais, lashed between two huge, curving rib bones that formed a grotesque arch, Ashe saw Constance. Arms pulled out sideways by ropes she slumped, head forward. Above her, where the bones had been lashed together, sat a hideous, three horned skull.

Ringing the circle of the living stood a circle of the dead. Human skeletons held upright by wooden stakes, bony feet resting on tiny, wooden platforms. Looking at them he remembered the ten-year-old nightmare of the skeletons that had loomed out of the fog. Ones similar to those he now looked at had probably been used, pushed forward by crawling Indians that day. The shock of seeing those terrible things had stopped Cal's heart all those years ago and left Ashe with a supernatural dread, only the dread had now been replaced with anger; anger at losing a good friend, anger at being made a fool of. It was time to redress the balance.

To the right he saw the others, the professor, Silas and the two brothers imprisoned in a bone cage. Silas was gripping the bone bars and staring out.

'This is insane, Grey Dog. We mean you no harm,' Silas's voice echoed clearly to Ashe.

'The spirits must be appeased. This sacred Shoshoni land, not for the white man. Spirits say all of you must die.' Grey Dog stood before the rock plinth on which the drummer sat beating out his monotonous dirge. 'When the light of the sun god touches the woman she will die. It is so written.'

Ashe looked, already the circle of light had reached the edge of the dais. He had to act now and quickly. A gun would have made things that much easier, but all he had was a knife and surprise.

The tunnel mouth where Ashe crouched was

about twenty feet up. Just below it a narrow ledge angled down to a rock cluttered floor. It was dark enough here to enter the cavern without being seen. He scrambled down quickly and ghosted forward under cover of the rocks.

Constance, dry-mouthed, shook the hair from her eyes and watched the circle of light inch its way towards her. She knew that there would be no miracle to save her this time. Ashe was dead. She had heard his screams and seen Grey Dog smile. Tears filled her eyes as the circle of light caressed the base of one bone upright.

Ashe had got as close as he could. Midway between the circle of dead and circle of living, he crouched behind a rock. Sweat beaded his face. He took a firm grip on the knife handle, licked dry lips and moved.

The slow beat of the drum hid the stealthy slap of his boots from the seated Indian until the very last second. Ashe was almost upon him when the man turned his white-painted face, hand straying to the Winchester at his side. His eyes opened wide at the sight of the white man, but his throat opened wider as the knife blade slashed deeply across it.

The Indian lurched to his feet, hands scarlet, blood jetting between his fingers as he tried to close the gaping wound. Ashe dived on the rifle, tossing the knife aside as the dying Indian reeled to one side, colliding with a rising partner. Ashe counted seventeen Indians including Grey Dog. As he came up in a crouch the Winchester roared in his hands as he levered and fired, levered and fired. Three

Indians went howling to the ground.

Panic reigned as the rest scattered for safety, the echoes of the gunshots crashing about the cavern. Panic was his only ally as he ran crab-like towards Constance. Once they had recovered from the shock of his arrival the boot would be on the other foot, so he had to make the most of his entrance. Constance stared at Ashe in open-mouthed disbelief, Grey Dog with a look of supernatural awe.

In a far corner of the cavern rock fragments and dust fell from the roof.

'You are dead,' Grey Dog said hoarsely.

The Winchester spoke again. The drummer screamed above the rolling thunder of the shot as the bullet smashed into his chest and threw him from the rock plinth. There was a meaty crunch as his body hit the floor.

'Folks have sure been trying to convince me of that lately,' Ashe replied with a grim smile. He thrust the end of the barrel under Grey Dog's chin. 'Make sure your braves know you get the next bullet if'n they try anything.' Ashe had moved to get the old man's body between himself and any bullets that might start flying.

Grey Dog screeched something in his own tongue before looking at Ashe.

'You will never leave the House of Bones,' he intoned darkly.

'Then we'll go t'hell together, old man,' Ashe hissed and pulled a knife from Grey Dog's belt. 'Now move with me, old man.' He edged towards

Constance. 'Need any help, ma'am?' he called lightly.

'You ever thought of taking up the rescue business professionally, Ashe?' she asked huskily.

'No, ma'am. Seems a mite too dangerous to my way of thinking.' Keeping the end of the rifle under Grey Dog's chin Ashe slashed the bonds that held her.

Stones rattled in another corner. High up a cloud of dust layered the beam of sunlight.

Keeping Grey Dog as a shield, Ashe and Constance moved to where the others were imprisoned. Rope fastened the door in place. Ashe gave the knife to Constance and seconds later the rest of the group had joined them.

'Isn't this place wonderful, Ashe?' The professor enthused with a joy that had Ashe staring suspiciously at him.

'Depends on which side you're on, Professor. For myself I just want to put as much space between it an' me as possible.' His eyes fell on Michael Boyde. Though white faced there was animation in the youngster's face. 'You OK, boy?'

'Got a bit confused back there, but I'm OK now.'

'I don't know how you managed it, Ashe, but the way Grey Dog explained it you shouldn't be here now,' Silas cried.

'Guess this old coyote got confused some too.'

'But, Ashe, you don't understand,' the professor broke in. 'This cavern represents the biggest and finest collection of dinosaur remains ever found. Dozens of species, millions of years old. It's the greatest archaeological treasure of all time.'

'That's as maybe, but if Grey Dog's boys get the chance your bones'll end up with the rest.' He eyed Grey Dog. 'Move it, old man, get us out of here an' maybe you'll live.'

Grey Dog eyed him sullenly then turned abruptly, throwing his arms in the air and yelling something in his own tongue. Ashe saw the white shapes of the painted Indians exchange glances. Grey Dog yelled again and Ashe had a premonition of what was coming next.

'Get down!' he yelled and dragged Constance to the floor.

A fusillade of shots rang out from a dozen or so weapons and bullets ploughed destructively into the old man's body. Grey Dog was lifted off his feet and thrown backwards in a welter of blood; he had deliberately given his life in order that they should not escape.

As the sound of the shots echoed and reverberated around the great cavern, Ashe crawled up behind a rock and threw a couple of quick shots at the darting, white figures.

Near the centre of the cavern a stalactite fell from the shadow hung roof, shattering noisily as it hit the floor. A second crashed down as the echoes of the first died away. Behind him Ashe heard the clatter of falling stones mingled with the crash of heavier rocks. Dust filled the beam of sunlight and spread outwards in a choking cloud.

A coldness filled the pit of Ashe's stomach. He had seen gunshots start avalanches and guessed the same was happening here.

'This whole place is gonna collapse any second,' he bawled. 'Which way's out?'

'We were brought in over there.' Silas jabbed a finger.

Constance screamed as a white shape appeared on the rock above Ashe. Ashe threw himself to one side, rolled on his back levelling and firing the rifle in a single move. The figure disappeared, its head exploding in a blossom of red.

'Lead the way, Silas and let's make it quick.' Ashe came to his feet as all around them the cavern began to emit loud, harsh cracking sounds of rock under tremendous pressure.

'But this is a disaster,' the professor wailed.

'So is getting squashed under a few thousand tons of rock,' Ashe replied and half dragged the professor by his good arm in the wake of the others.

Like spearheads from hell the stalactites fell from the roof to disappear into the rising cloud of dust, but making their presence known by a thunderous, shattering crash. The huge prehistoric animal remains that had survived for thousands of years were crushed and splintered beneath tons of rock and the ground shook beneath their feet. Frank Boyde had the presence of mind to snatch up a torch as he led the way with Silas and Michael. Constance followed while Ashe and the professor brought up the rear. Fragments of rock showered down on them as the dust thickened, biting into eyes and lungs.

It seemed to Ashe to take an eternity of blind stumbling through the choking darkness, following a dim, ethereal glow before entering a small, outer cave where the others waited. The dust was not so thick here and Ashe felt a surge of joy as he spotted the guns the group had carried and his own gunbelt tossed to one side.

'It's this way,' Silas shouted above the rumble of falling rock, indicating an opening ahead.

'Keep going, I'll be following,' Ashe replied as he paused to retrieve his gunbelt. The cavern belched dust into the cave as Ashe made his exit. For ten minutes he worked his way down a tunnel that in places had him crouched double, following the sounds of the others and finally the way ahead grew lighter.

Ashe emerged into glaring sunlight where the others were sprawled on the red sand coughing the dust from their lungs and wiping grit-filled eyes. He went to his knees coughing and spluttering. When he had recovered enough to take an interest in their surroundings he sat back on his haunches and looked around.

They had emerged into a wide, steep-sided gorge, the red cliffs forming a semi-circle about them. Half a mile ahead the gorge opened into a desert of red sand beyond which lay a further wall of red rock. Much, much closer loomed the grinning face of Scar. Constance screamed!

Scar placed the tip of his lance against Ashe's throat.

'The Great Spirit smiles on me,' Scar hissed. 'It

brings you to me, Ashe.' A trickle of blood ran down Ashe's neck as the tip of the lance broke skin. 'Twice you escape from me, but not this time.' Scar pulled the lance back and Ashe rubbed his neck. Scar had some ten men with him, hard-faced, seasoned warriors.

'Breaking your own traditions, Scar? Stepping on sacred ground.'

'I am Scar and even the demons bow to me.' His dark eyes bored into Ashe. 'I hear the mountains growl. Where is Grey Dog?'

'Visiting his ancestors.'

A thin, cold smile puckered the mutilated flesh of Scar's face.

'You shall join your's, Ashe.' Scar raised the lance.

A single shot rang out. Scar jerked as though he had been kicked in the back. A ragged hole spraying blood and bone fragments opened over his heart. Heads, white and red turned as Scar toppled forward. Ashe threw himself to one side, clawing the Colt Lightning from its holster that had been half buried in the sand beneath his right leg. He rolled over to his stomach triggering shots at the nearest Indians. Two went down. Ashe caught the sound of a bugle above the crash of shots as into the mouth of the gorge swept a tide of blue.

The remaining Indians threw down their weapons and drew into a silent group. Ashe came to his feet. A lone figure, well ahead of the cavalry troop, drew his horse to a slithering halt. Sheriff Clem Peters, a smile on his moustachioed face and rifle in his hand, leapt from the saddle.

'Figured you might need some help, Ashe.'

Ashe touched his fingers to his forehead in a salute.

'No, I had it all under control, Clem,' he replied with a broad, relieved smile. 'What the hell are you doing here?' He gripped the lawman's hand in a shake as the others gathered around.

'Seems old Scar went too far. Major got orders to get him and as I was the only one left who knew the area, I've been their unofficial guide. Been tracking him for a few days now. Had a few run-ins and these are all that's left.' He indicated the dejected Indians that the soldiers were rounding up. 'By the way, found your horse a-ways back, so figured you were somewhere close by.'

'You sure are a sight for sore eyes, Sheriff,' Silas said.

'Glad to be around when I'm needed,' Clem acknowledged.

'Lost, all lost,' the professor wailed looking as dejected as the captured Indians.

'No, we ain't lost, Professor,' Clem corrected.

'Ain't us he's worried about, Clem. Just some old pile of bones the mountain swallowed,' Ashe replied with a grin.

'Not just any old bones, Ashe.' The professor shook his head sadly.

'Well I might jus' have something for you as a keepsake,' Ashe replied mysteriously. Their eyes followed him as he returned to the tunnel entrance and retrieved something from the sand. It was a long-snouted, reptilian skull, twice the size of a human skull. The professor's eyes popped with joy as the skull was thrust against his chest and he wrapped his good arm about it.

'Ashe, this is marvellous. Silas, come take a look.'

'What the hell sorta critter is that?' Clem mouthed.

'Not the sort you'd wanna meet on a dark night that's for sure,' Ashe laughed.

Constance came over and took Ashe aside.

'That was a nice thing you did, Ashe. You're a kind man.'

Ashe looked shocked.

'Just as long as you don't tell anyone else, ma'am. Remember, I've gotta live here.'

They both laughed.

Later, as they rode from the canyon, Ashe felt contentment. A nightmare that had haunted him for ten years had finally been laid to rest.